The Legacy of Molly Southbourne

D0980149

ALSO BY TADE THOMPSON

THE MOLLY SOUTHBOURNE SERIES
The Murders of Molly Southbourne
The Survival of Molly Southbourne

THE WORMWOOD TRILOGY
Rosewater
The Rosewater Insurrection
The Rosewater Redemption

Making Wolf
Far from the Light of Heaven

THE LEGACY OF
MOLLY SOUTHBOURNE

TADE THOMPSON

A TOM DOHERTY ASSOCIATES BOOK
NEW YORK

This is a work of fiction. All of the characters, organizations, and events portrayed in this novella are either products of the author's imagination or are used fictitiously.

THE LEGACY OF MOLLY SOUTHBOURNE

Cover photo © Nilufer Barin/Arcangel Images
Cover design by Christine Foltzer

Edited by Carl Engle-Laird

A Tordotcom Book
Published by Tom Doherty Associates
120 Broadway
New York, NY 10271

www.tor.com

Tor® is a registered trademark of Macmillan Publishing Group, LLC.

ISBN 978-1-250-82471-4 (ebook)
ISBN 978-1-250-82470-7 (trade paperback)

First Edition: 2022

To Aliette,
my earliest adopter

At first I started back, unable to believe that it was indeed I who was reflected in the mirror.

—Mary Shelley,
Frankenstein

The Legacy of Molly Southbourne

One

Noel Berg sings aloud to keep himself awake. Something about driving makes him sleepy. Perhaps the vibrations, perhaps the drone of the engine, perhaps some memory of childhood, of sleeping in the car while his father takes the family somewhere. It's dark, the middle of the night. He sees few other cars on this country road. He sings Black Sabbath and eats crisps, his strategy for staying awake. The crunchiness is the key factor, the noise of them breaking apart in his mouth, and the action of pushing against resistance. He should use carrots. Healthier. But that requires the kind of planning Noel is not interested in undertaking.

A tire blows. The noise, the swerving of the car, the *whut-whut-whut-whut* of the crumpled rubber tortured by the rims, all make his heart sink. He hasn't changed a tire in years, and he is so out of shape that he'll probably cock it up. But he's going to do it because he is too ashamed to call a breakdown service for a flat tire. He brings the car to a stop with a soundtrack of Ozzy Osbourne screeching, and he is grateful that the road is empty.

He kills the engine, disengages his seat belt, and leaves the car. Quiet. Blood rushing in his ears, of course. All he can smell is exhaust and burned rubber from the tire on the road. He touches the asphalt to see if it retains heat from the day's sunlight. It doesn't.

It's past midnight, the sky a dark blue with stars that he usually would not see with the light pollution. The tree-tops delineate what he can and cannot see of the Milky Way. Below that line, darkness. Stupid. He returns to the car and turns on the engine, puts on the hazard lights. He pops the trunk and applies the wedges to the other wheels then loosens the lug nuts on the flat one.

He hears something crackle, like potato crisps crunching. He straightens up and turns on the headlights. Nothing. He listens, stops breathing. Nothing. He positions the jack and starts rotating. He stops and straightens up. This time he definitely heard something.

He turns around just in time to catch a brief movement, then his head flowers in stars as he is knocked off his feet. He does not cry out. Noel maintains awareness for a long time, while something impacts with his body, shaking his vision, all accompanied by Ozzy and electric guitar.

He knows he is paralyzed.

He knows he is dying.

Two

Myke finishes her cigarette, kills the end between finger and thumb, drops the stub, and stamps it out. She inspects the ground for embers and smoke. Satisfied, she starts jogging back. She does not tax herself, just takes it slow and steady. She only recently restarted running since she had a march fracture in the months before. Her GP seems to think she might be showing early signs of osteoporosis, which mortifies Myke. Not that she minds being middle aged, it's just that she has taken care of her body and cannot bear for it to start breaking down.

She looks for the markers, the branch configurations, the arrangements of stones and rocks, the twists in the path that tell her where she is. This is not a familiar route. It is Myke's habit to test herself by running down unknown walkways. Keeps the mind engaged. It's cloudy, a dense uniform cover that shouts the probability of rain, and in a corner of her mind she remembers flood warnings. But not for here. She speeds up, trying to find her limit. Her running shoes need replacing.

She passes a farm where cows chew the cud, indolent,

uncaring. The smell of their shit is on the wind. It doesn't bother Myke. She likes farms. She frightens a corvid who is eating something dead. Her approach used to be quieter. She used to be one with nature, swallowed up and accepted by the birds and the animals and the insects. *I am no longer a gazelle.*

She comes up to and crosses an A road without getting killed. In the UK you can pick up and eat roadkill as long as you didn't hit the animal yourself. Not her, not today. She plans to leap over the tributary of a stream, but mistimes it and gets her left shoe wet.

In half an hour, she is home. Small cottage, nearest neighbor half a mile away, lots of field space around. She keeps no animals because she has no desire to put them down when their time comes. She has killed enough in her lifetime.

She takes the shoe off and leaves it outside to dry. The phone is ringing as she comes in. She knows who it is and rushes to pick it up. She should really get a mobile phone one of these days.

"Yes?"

Too late, but she sees the answering machine flashing. She listens while she takes off her exercise clothes.

"Hi, Myke! It's Carol. Just a reminder for tonight: don't be late. You have to bring the crisps. Dip is optional, and disgusting if you ask me. We're doing Romero. I know, I know, Henry insists. He's found this Italian cut that has seven extra minutes in the mall or something. It was your idea to invite him to the club. See ya."

Myke hadn't forgotten. She showers, dresses, snatches the keys from her dresser, and leaves in her jeep. She stops at a convenience store to buy crisps. She doesn't eat them and doesn't know which are good, so she picks a few bags at random. Likewise the dip. The girl at the counter is rapt, listening to someone on television.

". . . that you are the architect of your life, that you determine what happens to you, and that you are responsible for your achievements. Not your god, not the government, not your parents, not your friends. You. I . . ."

Myke pays, puts the bag of goodies on the passenger seat, and speeds off to Carol's. Judging from the cars in the gravel driveway she is the last to arrive. This is usual. One of her friends once said she is consistently late because she doesn't really want to be there. Myke thanked her for the pop psychology and laughed ha-ha, but it was true then and is true now. She keeps it up because she has to be . . . normal. Tuesday night movie club is normal. Salt and vinegar crisps that Henry is going to hate, that is normal. Ergo, Myke is normal.

Her shoes outside the car, on the gravel. Crunch. Myke picks up the footsteps of another. There's a man standing beside one of the other vehicles. Myke looks everywhere else and sees nothing, but that doesn't matter. He might have backup skulking.

"Come out where I can see you," says Myke. "Or I'm calling the police."

"You don't have a mobile phone," says the man. Familiar voice. He puts his hands up all the same, and walks into the light shining from the front room window.

"Gove?"

"Hullo, Myke."

She hasn't cast eyes on him in years, although they spoke on the phone more recently than that. He is rounder, grayer, still wearing rumpled clothes, cheap suit, cheap tie, satchel across his chest, squinting because he is too self-conscious to wear glasses. His good deeds have balanced out his fuck-ups, enough for her to give him an audience. For now.

"Get into my jeep or we'll be seen."

They sit. He smells the way he always smells, musty, like libraries, like museums when Myke was a little girl. She always thought him sweet, too sweet for the business he is in. Must be protective coloration, because he never hesitated to make hard decisions or screw people over when the situation called for it.

"Gove, why are you in the field?" says Myke. She does not look at him. Through the window she watches Henry fiddle with his television set. If she knows him he'll be telling everybody about the amazing clarity of the picture, laced with technical stuff that Myke has never cared about. She still considers a color TV a luxury.

"It's nice to see you, Myke. Things have gone a bit downhill since we last spoke. The home secretary shrunk the department, echoes of the Wall coming down. They believe the war is won, taking their cue, as usual, from the Yanks."

"Clinton?"

"The long and short is they have to worry about Bosnia, Kosovo, China's military buildup, India and Pakistan at each other's nuclear throats, and a Congress that wants results from the War on Drugs. Narcotraficantes. The Cold War is won, yesterday's news, therefore yesterday's funding."

Myke turns to him. "What's the manpower like?"

"You mean including me?"

"Yes."

"One."

"What?"

"I'm a caretaker, Myke. A pilot light. Theoretically, they expect me to call for help if I need anyone. Use contractors and the like, Gove. We'll come running, old chap, don't worry. In practice, they're telling me to be a good sport and die quietly."

He can't mask the bitterness or the exhaustion in his voice.

"Why are you here, Gove?"

"I want to show you something." He opens the satchel and pulls a folder. There are computers for filing now, portable ones too, but Gove will always be a pen and paper man. He might use a typewriter, if he's feeling adventurous, but he wouldn't trust an electric one. Myke turns on the interior light and tries not to stare at the shiny patches of his threadbare suit.

He gives Myke a photograph of a man, head-and-shoulders shot, white, in this thirties, good haircut, smiling at the camera with confidence.

"Ever seen this man before?" asks Gove.

"Never."

"Sure?"

"I don't forget faces and you know it."

"That's Noel Berg. He's a car salesman, from Dumfries originally. Thirty-two, wife, two children, third on the way." He takes that picture and hands over a second one. Berg is lying on the side of a road, eyes open, dead, blood on his clothes, crime scene markers visible on the ground. There's a car in the background. "This was taken last week. His neck was snapped before all the other damage was done, which the postmortem ghouls say means he didn't feel the pain. The fatal blow was to his lower sternum. The lower part of it, the zyfi . . . zy . . ."

"Xiphisternum."

"That's the one. I can never quite say that word. They found it driven into his left ventricle, say that killed him, though they said if he had lived any longer he wouldn't have been able to breathe due to the broken neck. At this point they started arguing with each other. One doesn't think of forensic pathologists as passionate."

"It wasn't me, Gove. This is sloppy overkill, not a professional's work. This is a cruel—"

Gove shakes his head. "That's not what I think, and not why I'm here, although when the alert came across my desk I thought of the rather short list of people I know who can do that kind of thing. No, this is why I'm here." He shows her a third photo, which he lays over the one in her hand. She raises her thumb to accommodate it. Grainy. A night shot, and from the angle it looks like it was taken from the parked car in the first picture. Berg is already lying on the ground. Crouched over him, long wiry limbs with bare flesh, hair framing her face—

It can't be.

"That's a Molly Southbourne." Myke moves her thumb from side to side, rubbing the surface of the photo, as if she is trying to expose it as a fake.

Gove doesn't say anything at first. He flips off the light.

"How did you get this?"

"Being a salesman, Berg's car came with all the trimmings. There's a new thing with radar and a camera that switches on when you reverse. The car sloped downhill, so he had it in reverse while changing a tire. We pulled the image from there."

Myke is shaking with anger. "Gove."

"I know."

"I told you, I *warned* you that the girl you had in Shepherd's Bush wasn't Molly."

"I know, Myke."

"That's not an explanation."

"What can I say? She slipped through our fingers. We called her in and she rabbited. She tried to come in once after that, but we think she was kidnapped by another girl like her, Tamara Koleosho. There was a firefight when the agents tried to neutralize her. We got dozens of Koleosho corpses, but no molly."

Myke looks at the photo again. The face is calm, just as Myke would expect. *Good girl*?

"This doesn't make any sense. Mollies don't kill civilians who don't try to kill them first. We're sure Berg didn't try anything?"

"No. It looks like the molly emerged from the woods, killed Berg, then went back the way she came. There are footprints. They don't go far."

"Nothing in Berg's background?"

"Clean. He is, was, a civilian."

"Where was this murder done?"

"Just outside Okehampton."

"What the bloody hell is she doing in Devon?"

"Could it be an old one? Drifted south, lived off the land."

"I suppose so. What do you want from me?"

"You know what I want."

"Fine. Do you have a budget for this?"

"A thin one. I . . . we have assets that Whitehall doesn't know they know about. Make this simple and quick. Go to Devon, find the molly, neutralize it. Be subtle, Myke, we don't have cleanup on this. Obs-16 is dead, so if you make a mess housekeeping is on you."

"I'm subtle."

"You *can* be subtle."

Laughter surges from the house and the nature of the light on the blinds changes to the bluish glow of television. Myke hates watching in the dark. She hands the photos back.

"I'll need to take leave from my job," she says.

"I'll sort that out. You just pack and find that molly."

"I'll need some juice, something to protect me from the local Bobbies."

He reaches into the satchel again and emerges with ID for Myke.

"How did you know I'd say yes?"

"Because you hate the mollies and would exterminate

them for free if I asked nicely."

Myke nods.

"Give me regular updates. I want to hear from you every day."

"People who say that never receive updates, Gove. Now, get out of my car."

She turns on the engine and drives off, watching him in the rearview mirror.

Three

Tamara inhales with her nose and exhales with her mouth to calm the monkeys in her mind. She prefers the seiza position, kneeling, rump on ankles, hands on lap facing down, for meditation. She knows there are eyes on her.

She is in Samoa, hot, humid, and in some respects perfect for the event. She is here for hyakunin kumite, the Hundred-Man Kumite. People stare at her because she is a woman and because she is black, but mostly because nobody has heard of her. She is fine with that. Her biggest problem is that her karate background is in Shotokan. Hundred-Man is a Kyokushin thing. Still. She wants to do this.

She is meditating because that's all there is left to do, and because she is afraid. She has already had all these fights, these sparring sessions in her head. She has trained, and she has fought one hundred opponents, but those opponents happen to be herself, a hundred bodies with the same skill, same . . . instincts.

A breeze ruffles her gi, but it is warm and does nothing to alleviate her sweatiness.

As always, when she thinks of combat she visualizes Molly Southbourne. Molly tried to make Tamara unlearn karate, a martial art inadequate for self-defense in the real world in Molly's opinion. Molly's art was a mishmash, cobbled from systema, jiu-jitsu, taekwondo, wushu, boxing, wrestling, anything that had to do with subduing an opponent.

When they fell out, Tamara rededicated herself to karate. She still maintains the skills of other disciplines, and she had some of the tamaras become experts in specific fields to teach the rest of them.

She has to remember to stick to the rules of karate. Tamara traveled twenty-three hours from London to Apia. She has not come to fail. In hindsight she should have come here earlier to acclimatize.

"Miss Koleosho?"

She opens her eyes. A Samoan man in a black belt and white gi is standing there, smiling. Lots of smiles in Samoa. She asked about this and was told it is faa Samoa, the Samoan way.

"Yes?"

"I am to remind you that you have one hundred fights lasting ninety seconds each. You have to win at least half of them."

"All right."

"Also, that no woman has ever completed this. The

judges were quite insistent that I tell you this."

"Thank you for telling me. I'm sure they'll be perfectly objective."

"Will you follow me?"

Not much of a crowd. The combatants stand easy in ranks to her left. Quick multiplication of rows versus columns tells her there aren't one hundred people, but she knows that some will come around several times.

The sempai calls out instructions.

"Komaite, sensei ni rei."

She prepares, then bows to the judges.

"Otagai ni rei." She bows to the combatants.

She hopes they don't ask her to perform kata as a warm-up. Just get to the fighting, please.

The first opponent steps up, they bow, and face off. Tamara doesn't wait. Where other fighters would be range-finding and spirit-testing, she feints with a front kick and swivels into a reverse kick that knocks him off his feet, face contorted in pain. She returns to a fighting stance and waits for the next, jubilation coiling and flexing inside her.

A thin man steps in; bows to her.

Tamara bows . . .

~

She wins thirty-one. It is not enough.

Her preparation over the last nine months, her training, her near starvation, her deprivation, futile. She fights seventy fights before collapsing into exhaustion. She wins thirty-one. She only wins thirty-one.

By the seventy-first fight she no longer knows where she is. Her arms feel like they are strapped to giant logs of wood, and she can't keep them up. Her head wants to fall off her shoulders. She reaches an out-of-body state that makes her doubt her own identity. She seems to be watching the humiliation from far away.

She cannot go further. Her lungs, her heart, her muscles, they all tell her to quit or die, and Tamara is not prepared to die for this.

After, she suffers the condescending never-minds, the you-fought-with-honors, the reminders that no woman has won before and experts do not think it possible.

She sleeps for two days, prepares for home, and flies back to London via New Zealand, Hawaii, Los Angeles. On the plane she watches a dinosaur film called *Jurassic Park*. She finds it diverting, but her defeat creeps around the edges of the screen.

There is a tamara waiting for her at arrivals.

She sits silently as the tamara drives her home. Her entire body throbs, four days after the last fight.

"Is there anything we need to know?" says Tamara.

"Vitali is looking for us," says the tamara.

"He can speak to any one of us."

"He says he wants you, the Prime. I told him we don't recognize those distinctions anymore, but he seemed unimpressed. What do you want to do?"

Vitali Ignatiy Nikitovich is an old Soviet, a conspiracy theorist who had an affinity for Molly Southbourne's mother. He was a mentor figure for Tamara, sort of, but she is dubious of him now. He may still be loyal to the Soviets, or what's left of them, and is trying to get Tamara to give him one of her clones. She hired two out and Vitali used them to guard two damaged mollies. Molly made short work of the tamaras when she found her wounded sisters.

"We're watching him?" says Tamara.

"Of course. He is in Milton Keynes, in a hotel by Willen Lake."

"We'll pay him a visit. Drive north on the M1."

~

Our name is Tamara Koleosho, and we are many.

Right now there are seventeen of us, though we're getting that itch in the base of the brain that means number eighteen is most likely coming soon.

We are, at present, spread over a two-mile radius, mostly in Milton Keynes. We are accountants, road workers, occupational therapists, admin managers, childminders, surgeons, police officers, taxi drivers, retail workers, cleaners, call center workers, salespeople, and unemployed. We are all that.

When we sit on a park bench in Willen Lake a few minutes after midnight, we are not surprised when Vitali Ignatiy Nikitovich shuffles up and sits next to one of us. It may well be that Vitali knows more about us than we do ourselves. Seeing him often means trouble.

"Tamara," he says.

"Vitali," we say.

"You've been difficult to find."

"We've been busy living, Vitali."

He nods. He is a bearded, older man, Russian, but been around England and Wales for years now. The world has shown its disdain for this kind of warrior, and the effect is obvious. The fabric of his clothes is unraveling, his shoes tired and on the verge of collapse, the tobacco he rolls, cheap.

"How was Japan? I heard. The Hundred-Man is not for a woman."

"It was Samoa, and it will be."

"Perhaps. Tell me, Tamara, have you seen Molly?" He says it casually, as if that's not been the only thing on his mind.

The last time we heard from Molly Southbourne it

was a phone message, and it scared us out of our fucking clothes.

You know who this is. You also know by now that I know all of your plans and I want no part of them. If you let this go, I will, and we can all get what we want. If you try to follow me or impede me in any way I promise you, I will murder you all. Test me, and see.

We had and have no desire to test her. We had an idea she went south; we moved in the opposite direction.

"No," we say. "And fuck you for bringing it up."

"We need a Molly Southbourne, Tamara."

"'We' don't need anything. You and we have no common cause, Vitali."

"You owe me."

"We do not."

"All right, let me say this another way, Tamara Koleosho. I have helped you. I am asking for your help."

"With what?"

"Like I said, we need a Molly Southbourne. We need to get one of her out of the country. Help me in this, and we will part ways forever."

"No. You will pay us, because someone is paying you for this service."

"Does it look like I am in a position to pay anyone, Tamara Koleosho?"

"Does it look like we care?" We get up and walk away

from him, knowing it is not the last time we will see him, knowing that this is just an opening gambit.

Already, though, we begin to plan, theoretically, how we might subdue Molly Southbourne. In some scenarios she lives, in others she dies, and in all of them, the cost to us is great.

If you try to follow me or impede me in any way I promise you, I will murder you all. Test me, and see.

All.

The wise thing might be to run.

"Tamara," says Vitali from behind us.

We turn.

"I'll pay you."

We nod.

"The molly can't be injured. Unconscious is fine, but no brain damage. No cuts. It can't be burned or otherwise traumatized."

"What about the watchers? Obs-16." We are mindful that the organization is looking for us and others like us.

"They will not be a problem. Trust me on that."

"Then we're in business." We sit back down to talk money and terms. We wonder who he represents, but if it's a foreign power it's likely to be Russia. They say the USSR is gone. Tamara knows that governments come and governments go, but intelligence agencies abide. They just change uniform.

Four

In her seat by the window Molly Southbourne, now known as Molly Whitlow, has a view of the yard and the trees that line it. She sees Moya stuck there, staring at something, but not moving. She is hooded, as always, and wears dark glasses, not against the glare, but because of the damage to her eyes. The afternoon sun excites the butterflies and makes the grass seem greener, the sky bluer.

Moya is too frightened to go into the woods. It took months to get her outside the house. Molly is proud of her progress.

Inside the room, Molina is talking.

"I cannot look at her without experiencing rage in the deepest part of myself. I have tried not to. I know what she has done for me." She turns to Molly. "I know what you've done for me, and I love you. But yours is the face of death."

"We have the same face," says Molly.

"Why do you think I have no mirrors in my room?"

Molina and Molly look like identical twins. Ann, or Mollyann, looks like their sister, with a withered hand she keeps strapped to her body. Moya, who is outside, is badly burned and keeps her appearance hidden. She has no hair on her head, and one eye has no lids. She does not talk.

The fourth person in the room is a private therapist, Dr. Song Ling, and to Molly she looks confused. Understandable. They can't tell her everything, and she's a professional. She senses gaps in the story, no doubt. From her perspective, she is dealing with signs of trauma, bad dreams in Molina, and serious interpersonal conflict between Molly and Molina.

Living with Moya, Ann, and Molina is difficult for Molly. Molina was late for work one day, and when Molly went to wake her she broke Molly's nose. Then she visited sustained violence on Molly for at least two minutes. Molina was apologetic and mortified, blamed her violence on the nightmares. Being in the same room can be tense. Moya picks up on this and usually leaves the room. Any hint of an atmosphere and Moya gets seriously stressed. Molly tries to be strong for everybody, especially Ann, who is sweet, a hard worker at the self-defense studio. She has good cheer, though Molly can't tell where it comes from or if it's some kind of front.

Molly writes copiously in her journals, filling page after page with her observations, thoughts, and blank verse at times.

"Let's backtrack a bit," says Ling. "Molina, what's the one thing you would like to be solved here?"

"I'd like to not have to look at Molly."

"Would you like to move out?" asks Ling.

"No."

"Molly?"

"I have no plans to live elsewhere."

"Molina, who does Molly remind you of?" asks Ling.

"Molly."

"I mean, in your past. Does she look like your mother or father?"

"Mother."

"I see. Don't take this the wrong way, but did your mother abuse you?" asks Ling.

"No," says Molina.

"No," says Molly.

Ling turns to Ann and raises one eyebrow.

"She did," says Ann.

Molly does not want any information like this going to outsiders. She knew the risk, though. She can't help being mildly irritated at Ann for contradicting them.

"Physically?" asks Ling.

Ann nods.

"Sexually?"

Ann shakes her head.

"Emotionally?"

Ann is thoughtful. "She taught us violence, both in word and in deed. She assaulted us so that we would become tough. She imposed a view of the world on us, a fearful view, a view that instigates a violent defense. She was paranoid and made us paranoid. She thought she was preparing us."

"I see. Do you see your mother these days?" asks Ling.

Ann exhales, then says, "No, she's dead."

"How did she die?"

"She and my father were murdered," says Molina.

The therapist nods slowly. "I'm sorry to hear that."

Molina brushes this off with a wave of the hand. "It was a long time ago."

"Is it possible, Molina, that Molly reminds you of your mother?"

"Of course she does. They look alike. We all look alike."

"Then if that's the case, is it also possible that seeing her reminds you of the threat of seeing your mother, and you feel the need to defend yourself, ironically using the exact tools your mother gave you?"

"It's possible, I guess." Molina fiddles with a black bowler hat. She never wears it, just carries it around with her. It's Molly's hat, in point of fact, but Molina appropriated it.

"What did your father do while all this was going on?"

Molly flashes back to being tied up in a barn with two dead mollies on the floor, and her father pointing a gun at her head. She had just broken his jaw in three places and it was held in place by a bandage.

"My father was her reliable partner in this," says Molly. "They were one hundred percent in agreement."

"They were not," says Molina. She seems to have gelled her frizzy hair. "Pa had limits."

"But he never stopped her," says Ann.

"Is it possible that your mother was mentally unwell?" asks Ling.

"Why do you say that?" asks Molly.

"Because you've described having two episodes of psychosis, one when you were very young on a farm, and one when you went berserk and assaulted a whole bunch of people, including police officers."

"She wasn't psychotic," says Molly.

"And that there is my problem," says Molina. "Molly wants to be like her. She thinks Ma was right."

"Is that true, Molly?" asks Ling.

Molly swallows, throat suddenly feeling dry. "Dr. Ling, we were born in circumstances I can't tell you about, but they were unusual."

"I've seen cases like yours, multiple births from fertility treatment, before," says Ling.

"Not like us," says Ann.

"The point is, Moya and Ann were beaten and burned as ... the first thing they knew about life or living. They were kept in cages and brutalized. I rescued them using skills that I learned from ... my mother. Molina ... That's even more difficult to describe. She was an experiment, a horrific science project. I got to her because of my mother's training."

"You didn't free me," says Molina.

"No, I didn't. You freed yourself." To the doctor she says, "I am as my mother made me. We are here as a family now because of my mother."

"You were also endangered by your mother," says Ling. "If she didn't put you in danger, would you have needed all the skills she imparted to you?"

Molina and Molly exchange looks. If their mother hadn't encouraged killing the clones, they wouldn't have had to spend every day fighting to survive.

Don't bleed.

Those rules.

Those fucking rules.

Five

Myke drives out toward Colnbrook, then takes a side road, and another side road after an interval. The road is craggy, but the jeep can handle it, even towing a horse box.

She comes to a gated fence and stops. She gets out, opens the gate, gets back in, and drives on. There is distant thunder and dark gray on the horizon, but the sun is still shining in this part of the sky. Five more minutes of driving and the road opens up into the frontage of a building. It's a red pillbox, nondescript design, but a Brutalist influence if you squint. The roof has fans, large ones, which are also above the doors.

Myke knows that there are backup generators attached to the back of the building. She has only been here twice before. She half expected the building to be gone. The site has no name, just a designation. As a bookkeeper, Myke knows that when something is just a number in the accounts and it saps a lot of money, it's something illicit.

She parks. Not a single challenge. This place used to be more secure, but given what Gove told her, Myke decided to take a chance. The program can't police all their assets if they only have one person in charge.

She stretches and walks toward the front door. She is noting how the approach lacks weeds when the guard rounds the corner.

"Oi! Where do you think you're going?" he says.

"Oh, thank goodness. I thought this place was abandoned. Please, help me. I just left the house and drove away. I don't know where I am. He's trying to kill me." Myke runs toward the guard. He is taken aback. She twigs that he has no gun or truncheon, and the pepper spray on his belt is old. No body armor.

"Calm down, ma'am," he says.

"I am calm," says Myke.

She rakes her fingers across his eyes, kicks his crotch, then leaps on to his back, capturing his neck in the V of her elbow. He grunts, falls to his knees, struggles ineffectively. Myke kneels behind him, patient. You have to be with this kind of thing. He's a big lad and the feel of his body suggests he is not a stranger to resistance training. Can't go toe-to-toe with him at this weight difference, no matter how dismal his training.

He goes limp. She ties him up and drags him behind the building by the scuff of his shirt. Makes her breathless. She takes his bunch of keys and his passes. No radio. He's a lone shift worker, then.

The windows are all stained, so she can't see inside the building at this level.

She lets herself in the front door, which is unlocked. Inside, everything is white. Maybe it used to gleam, but now it's just dull, dirty and perverse. You can't decorate with white if you aren't going to maintain it.

She trots through the facility, unsure of when the guard will be relieved. There's a corridor and a staircase. She does a quick round of the ground floor. Offices, some locked, some not. That's not why she's here, so she goes up the stairs. The temperature drops considerably, and there's the hum of machinery. That's more like it.

The second floor is an open space, walls lined with refrigerated shelves. There are additional freestanding shelves with refrigerated compartments, thirty by fifty inches. The room is cold like a morgue.

Running through the likely keys, she opens some of the compartments and slides the drawers out. Dead bodies. Long dark hair, pale skin, toned muscle. All ages, but none older than thirty. Babies with crushed skulls, teenagers with collapsed rib cages. All of them are Molly Southbourne duplicates. The newest section has a black girl, same age, dead by violent means as well. Toe tag says Tamara Koleosho. Only about a hundred or so of her.

She checks her watch and starts working. First, she kills the power to the entire building. She extracts each body from its compartment, then dumps them in careless mounds of tangled limbs. When she is done her muscles tremble with fatigue and she is wet with sweat. She looks at the last molly out of the fridge and spits in its face. *Fuck you.* She heads back to her jeep for a break, sick of inhaling formaldehyde.

The top floor is a laboratory, full of specimen jars and files. Organ samples, analyses, reports. It takes fifteen minutes to find what she's looking for. She selects five specimens labeled "spleen" and takes them back to the jeep in organ carriers.

She opens the horse box and it is full of cylindrical petrol cans. She walks back and forth, leaving the cans open and on their side, leaking fuel.

Shouts from behind the building. Myke investigates.

The guard is awake now and baleful. "Ey, wot are you doin', then?"

Myke thinks of dousing him in petrol, but decides to give him a pass.

She lights the building on fire. She waits to make sure it spreads to the first and second floors. She disconnects the trailer and sets it ablaze.

She gives the guard one more look. She rubs her chin, goes to him, and crouches. The flames crackling this close are not as dangerous as the broken glass showering down at intervals.

"What do I look like?" asks Myke.

He says, "A woman in overalls."

She narrows her eyes. "What do I look like?"

"How should I know? I didn't get a good look, did I?"

"Good man." She rummages in his clothes till she finds some ID, which she takes with her.

She can see the smoke column all the way back to the M25 orbital motorway.

She has two more stops at Woking and Maidenhead. She leaves both sites in flames, body count zero.

Now that she has finished with the dead, it's time to call the quick to account.

Time to visit Devon.

She drives south.

Six

There is definitely somebody under those leaves, asleep, but also naked. Sean drops the binoculars and returns to the tent. He shakes Jane awake.

"What time is it?" she asks. This is what she always says when she wakes.

"I think there's a naked woman in the woods," Sean says.

"You see naked people everywhere," says Jane. She gets up, kisses him, and slips the binoculars off his neck. "Where?"

He points.

Jane scours the scene in front of her. Trees, brush, maybe a squirrel, no nudity.

"Show me," says Jane.

He looks, and there's no sleeping person. Huh. Where'd she go?

"She was just there," he says.

"You saw another camper, out for a morning shit. Speaking of which . . ."

It bothers Sean for half an hour, then he is absorbed in

reading the map and planning their hike. Maybe an hour passes before he realizes Jane hasn't returned.

"Jane. Jane!"

He goes looking. No success. He makes his way back to the tent in case he missed her on the trail. He sees movement and sighs with relief.

"I was worried for a moment there . . ." He opens the flap.

It's not Jane. A filthy woman, covered in mud and—is that blood? Naked. This is the woman he saw before. She looks feral. Her gaze is unblinking, her head unmoving. She's hunkered down, going through their things.

"Can I help you?" he says, and regrets it immediately. She is clearly mentally deranged and needs help. He doesn't know whose blood that is, but she isn't injured. "I'll get you something to wear, something of Jane's. Do you speak English?"

She doesn't move.

"I'll get a blanket," says Sean. He turns and she's on him. He would have thought there was enough space for him to escape if need be, but he misjudged her speed. He feels agonizing pain in his left shoulder joint, then the arm just flops. She has a handful of his hair and yanks his head back. Her elbow smashes into his nose. He takes a tumble and they both fall down an incline. He hits his head on a root and sees stars.

He comes to rest and finds blood on the leaves around him. It's not his. He follows the trail and it ends with Jane. He sobs. He doesn't need to touch her to know she is dead.

This time he does hear the sound and he turns into it.

A face contorted with rage, then nothing.

Seven

"No," says Molly.

"It'll be good for her," says Molina.

"We can't."

"Why not?"

"It isn't safe."

"For who?"

"We don't have passports," says Molly.

"We can get those. Come on. I bet France is awesome. I want to see where Leonardo da Vinci was born."

"He was born in Italy, Molina."

"I'm going to a travel agent. I think Moya needs to get out of this place. At least for a few weeks."

"Help me open the gym, you brat. Moya doesn't like changes of environment."

"She told you this?"

"No, but whenever we change something her behavior gets odd."

"I bet she'll talk in France. English is the problem. En Français, s'il vous plaît."

"That's all the French you know." Molly opens the

shop front. "We're not taking Moya out of the country. None of us is leaving the country. We're keeping a low profile."

"You have no love in your heart," says Molina. "The French understand love."

"Either help me or bugger off, Molina."

"All right, I'm going to work anyway."

Molly opens the gym and spends the day reading *The Idiot*. Very few people come in to work out, but her clients pay monthly, so she doesn't mind. Molly's also never surprised when her sister doesn't help. Molina can't stand violence at all. Molly herself doesn't train in the house or talk about anything that might upset her sisters.

Sisters. How easy it comes to her now, saying siblings, but they are duplicates. It's unspoken, but its presence in the room is elephantine.

She leaves the gym to the receptionist and takes a walk. The asphalt is wet from the brief shower earlier. She breathes deeply of the clean air. In spite of everything, she feels good, happy, content. Everybody's safe. Everybody's fed and nobody is at each other's throats. No boys sniffing around. No girls either. Molina takes her libido elsewhere, tomcats for about a week every month, then comes back, sated. Molly doesn't know where exactly she goes.

She wanders into the Royal Albert Memorial Museum and drifts, soaking everything in, listening to snatches of conversation from normal people. Ann draws and paints better than anyone; she would have liked this. When it comes to visual arts, Molly is middling at best.

She stops at a painting. *Golconda* by Magritte, 1953. Molly has seen it before, when it first arrived on loan from Texas. An oil painting of men in black bowler hats and dark overcoats floating against a background of terraced suburban town houses and a blue sky. At first glance the men seemed identical, and Molly thought to herself, *This is me, this is us.*

"They're not identical," Molina had said, and she was right. A closer look showed variations in the faces and even builds. Molly thinks of it often, feels unsettled by it, and bought a bowler hat, though Molina took it hostage and has never relinquished control.

Molly moves on, turning away from the painting, but...

She senses something wrong.

She immediately turns around and walks back to the gym. *If you are in danger and you're on unfamiliar ground, if possible get to a space you can control.*

What spooked her?

It might be familiar faces she picked up in the crowd,

which make her feel she is being watched or followed. Is that it? Or is she becoming psychotic again? Dr. Ling put her back on regular medication and Molly is taking it seriously.

She dismisses the receptionist for the day. She illegally blocks the fire exit with a chair. She inserts a mouth guard and she surrounds herself with items she can improvise as weapons. She waits, staring at the entrance, heart hammering.

She waits.

The phone rings a few times, but she lets it go to voice message.

She waits.

It grows dark.

Cautious, she opens the door and peers out. The high street is deserted, all other shops closed, some shuttered.

She goes back in, waits.

Around midnight a woman comes to the glass, holds her hands to the sides of her face to block out light so she can see better. It's Ann.

Later, at home, a mug of lemon tea in her hands, Ann ruffles Molly's hair.

"It happens to me too, Mol," says Ann.

Molly nods.

"I'm sure it happens to 'Lina."

"Yeah."

The windows seem threatening.

She lies down to rest, but she can't sleep. After an hour Moya comes into her room and hugs her. Listening to her sister's heartbeat, Molly drops off.

Eight

"What did you do?" asks Gove.

"Don't raise your voice at me," says Myke. "I know you're upset, and you have good reason, but I don't like people yelling at me."

The phone booth feels humid, like people had had sex in it, but Myke knows it's because of the rain. Wet homeless people fleeing downpours.

"You burned the buildings," says Gove.

"I did."

"All the samples."

"Samples? Is that what we're calling the mollies now?"

"Where do I begin?"

"Nowhere, because you have already begun. You can only begin once. I wish you would stop so we can talk of more productive things."

"You burned the buildings."

"You said that already."

"They represented years of work."

"Uh-huh."

"And I had to smooth it over with Fire, Police, and

Forest Enterprise."

"What the hell is Forest Enterprise?"

"They look after woodlands in England, woodlands that you endangered with this stunt. I didn't know they existed until today."

"There was enough concrete around the buildings to serve as a firebreak. I am a friend to nature and wildlife."

"Myke, sometimes embers get blown. But this is not the point. I have superiors. I can't help you if I get redeployed. Or fired. I can't pay you if this happens. I can't protect you."

"Take it easy, Gove. We're helping each other."

"You are not helping me when you light the sodding beacons of Gondor for the whole country to see. Low profile, Myke. Subtle. That's what we said, isn't it?"

"I can do subtle."

Gove sighs into the receiver. It sounds like a hurricane. "Listen, I know you hate the whole Molly Southbourne thing, but if your emotions are clouding this assignment, I can find somebody else."

"Gove, I am not clouded by emotion. I eliminated all the other mollies, and now all I have to do is find this one in Devon, eliminate it, and burn the organic matter with a thermite grenade. Then I'll be done."

"But those mollies were already dead."

"The existence of their cadavers was an insult to me. I

learned to live with it when the odds weren't good. With your budget being what it is . . ."

"We're not making progress, so I'm just going to leave it. Go and do your job, all right? Try not to make a mess. And give me *daily* updates."

"Goodbye, Gove." She hangs up.

She gets into the jeep and checks the map, plotting a route for Okehampton.

Nine

This is inconvenient, thinks Tamara.

The whole place is too white. We stand out, which means we can't search in the daytime, even though we know what to look for.

What would you do?

I have no marketable skills, Tamara, I can't do anything.

That's not true. You can teach self-defense and fitness. You can open a gym.

You think?

Yes. From that one thing, you get your others to learn new skills, and they bring income into the communal pot.

Mollies aren't like tamaras. Mollies are violent and recalcitrant. They don't obey.

You only think in terms of command, obedience, discipline, Molly. That's not the way. Become one. Make every single one of you the same person and there'll be no limit to what you can achieve.

I don't want that. I . . . we're individuals. We each have to live our lives.

Whether you're individuals or not, you're still going to

need to know how to run a business. So, let me introduce you to the joys of double-entry bookkeeping and why it changed the world as we know it.

I like how you get excited about accounts. You are not a nerd at all.

Fuck you, Southbourne. No supper for you.

Tamara drops the curtain. They did have their moments, she and Molly.

But now she has to find her. If Molly isn't making duplicates, there should only be three to deal with, and the two are injured, damaged in the fire that killed the first Molly. Those two won't be as dangerous. It's the Prime that's the problem.

And unlike before, Tamara isn't willing to lose any of herself.

She stays in the hotel, orders room service, watches films, waits. She is still recovering from the tournament and it hurts to sit down. She spends time recalling every conflict with Molly Southbourne, every sparring session, every observation. How the hell is she going to take a molly without shooting her?

When night comes, she walks to the town center, avoiding drunks and belligerent revelers. She checks every martial arts school and gym she can find. She looks up the names of the instructors in the Yellow Pages. It would be frustrating work for one person, but there are seventeen of her in eight different hotels. They make short work of it. In the car park of a pub the tamaras compare names and don't find any likely to be Molly, but it's not like they can tell from a list.

The next assignment is to eyeball these people, which they do the next day from rental cars with tinted windows.

No match. On to the next town.

They move from east to west, hitting towns like Bognor Regis, Colworth, Chichester, Havant, Southbourne—Southbourne! Surely...no—Eastbourne, Hayling Island, Waterlooville, Portsea, Southsea, Gosport...it goes on. They hop to Southampton, birthplace of the *Titanic,* scour Lyndhurst, search Bournemouth, then spend a week on the beach to catch their breath.

It is the kind of work that others would give up, but they are spelled by other tamaras, and are always fresh. Except, of course, for Tamara Prime.

Ten

"I have been able to say this, but I've never been able to satisfactorily explain it to anyone," says Molina. "Inside me, deep, beneath all the humanity, beneath civilization, beneath whatever it's called, the Lizard Brain, under all of that is a reservoir of anger and pain that churns and bubbles. It isn't normal anger. I've seen people get angry, and it just seems . . . cute. I've seen other people fighting. I've seen boxing matches and I've seen street fights. I've seen violent sex and sexual violence. People angry enough to shrug off social convention and let out the beast. I have never seen anything that comes even close to what I feel in myself. I'm frightened. I'm frightened that I will kill everybody."

"All your sisters?" says Ling.

"No, I mean everybody. Everybody in the world. I might begin here, move on into town, kill everybody, then keep killing my way across the world until an armed response unit kills me or I kill the last person and end the human race. Then, still in a rage, I'd kill myself."

"I can see why that would be frightening," says Ling.

"Have you ever heard the story of the happy hedge-hog?"

"Let's assume I haven't," says Ling.

"A very angry tailor, I don't know why he was a tailor, he just was, anyway, he gets angry at everyone, his kids, his wife, the man who delivers lettuce."

"There are people who deliver lettuce?" asks Molly.

"You're focusing on the wrong thing," says Molina. "The tailor gets so angry one day that he has to scream, but he's frightening everybody at home, right? So he goes to the beach one night and screams into the waves. The waves throw out a stoppered bottle. He pulls out the stopper and here's this genie. Genie grants him one wish."

"Not three?" asks Ann.

"Can I just tell my story? Grants him one wish and tells him not to push his luck. Guy wishes he can shape-shift into an animal. Genie says which animal, he says a hedgehog. Genie says that's fine. You can now change into a hedgehog if you say the word 'hedgehog.' To turn back to a human, you just say 'human.' Genie blows away. Tailor guy says 'hedgehog' and he is miraculously trans-formed into a hedgehog. He runs about on the beach sand, marvels at it, feels somewhat happy.

"But he can't change back to human form, because his brain has shrunk to the size of a hedgehog's and he can't remember what he was doing before. Plus his lips can't form the word 'human.' So he remains a hedgehog forever. A happy hedgehog. The end."

"I see. Molina, do you think that in order to be happy you have to somehow become less than yourself, your true self? Less than human?" asks Ling.

"Dunno. Maybe."

"Do you see the anger as something that's part of you, or as an intruder to be expelled?"

"Dunno. But I do know that arguing with Molly sometimes helps," says Molina, looking at her sister.

"Then argue with me. I can take it," says Molly. "If it makes you better, I'll gladly argue with you."

"But I don't really want to," says Molina. "I love you, and I can see myself arguing with you from the outside, and I feel myself wanting to punch your face in."

"Then punch my face in," says Molly. "I can take that, too."

The door opens and Moya stands there, face in the shadow of her hood. She points to the window. Molly rises and looks out.

There's someone in the yard, standing in Moya's spot.

"Is everything all right?" says Ling.

"Keep going, I'll be back."

Molly is aware of Moya trailing her as she skips out to the yard. The person is dressed in dirty baggy clothes that do not match.

She is also a molly.

They recognize each other at the same time. The molly widens her eyes and opens her mouth in silent rage. Behind and to the left, Moya moans.

Here we go again.

The molly lunges, fluid, fast. Molly shifts her head and whacks her jaw with an overhand right. She meets the molly's head with a left uppercut and side-kicks her exposed belly. Molly keeps herself at a distance, instead of landing a final blow. The molly is down, but not even close to being out.

"I am not your enemy. You are welcome here, but you have to calm down. I know you're confused, but I can't let you hurt my sisters." Molly hears Moya over her shoulder, whimpering. "Moya, get inside the house with the others. Go."

The molly stands, eyes on Molly, then glances to the left, like she's going for Moya. She feints, sending Molly in the wrong direction. The molly darts past, running toward the house. Fuck. Molly chases, barely able to keep up. She surges and slams her body into the duplicate, crashing both of them into the sandstone wall.

Molly swings and misses and the molly stamps on her knee, which drives her down. She can see the fist approach but can't do anything to stop it connecting with her nose. Molly falls to the grass and the molly follows, wanting to grapple. Mistake. Molly traps the molly's ankle by scissoring her own, then turns, breaking it. The molly screams.

"I'm sorry," says Molly. She punches the molly's lights out.

~

"You're limping," says Molina.

"I'm fine," says Molly.

"You're not fine. Clearly you're not fine. Ann, tell her she's not fine."

Ann gestures with her withered hand without looking. "Between you all."

"Thanks for that. Helpful," says Molina.

They're all staring at the new molly, trussed up, out cold, and in the guest bed.

"Where the fuck did this one come from?" asks Molly.

"I see you gave her a traditional Southbourne welcome," says Molina.

"She was going to hurt Moya," says Molly. Defensive.

"Do you think Moya is unable to handle herself?" asks Molina. "You do remember that we all share memories?"

"Moya hasn't been training. This is a molly. You can't just subdue one with . . . Listen, why don't you make yourself useful?"

"I have. I stalled Dr. Ling and kept her from observing your fight. I was on the verge of faking a seizure," says Molina.

"Why is there a new molly?" asks Ann.

"I don't know," says Molly.

"And why is the new molly here?" asks Ann.

Molina points to Molly. "They are drawn to her. That's why she didn't kill Moya in the yard."

"She did go after Moya."

"Later. That was strategic," says Molina. She kneels on the bed.

"Careful . . ." says Ann.

"It's fine," says Molina. She studies the molly's nails, hair, teeth. "She's not new."

"Why do you say that?" asks Molly.

"New mollies have these transverse lines across their nails, growth lines that correspond to whatever materials they built themselves from. It takes six months to grow the nail out, for the line to disappear. This molly is older than six months."

"How do you know this?" says Ann.

"I don't want to say. It's gross," says Molina.

"Don't tell me . . ."

"I have James Down's memories from when I was . . . inside him."

"I said not to tell me," says Molly. "Jeez. Nobody wants

to be reminded of that."

"What do we do with her?" asks Ann.

"We teach her love, not aggression," says Molly.

"And if she can't be taught?" asks Molina.

"I taught you, didn't I?"

"By breaking every bone in my body."

"No, just two. You're so dramatic." She sits down in an armchair opposite the bed. "We take turns watching her. I'll go first."

When the others have gone Molly settles in for a long haul. She wonders if this was what she thought was wrong the other time. If the mollies can pick up a signal from her, can she pick one up from them? Is there a way for her to neutralize the signal she sends? Should she even want to? If there are more mollies out there making their way to her, shouldn't she help them come home? She can welcome them, look after them here.

At some point during the night she senses Moya hovering, then disappearing.

The molly wakes up. She immediately begins straining toward Molly, pulling against the restraints, veins standing out like ropes on her neck. Her face is a mask of hate blotched with swellings and bruises from their conflict.

"I'm sorry I hit you," says Molly. "You left me no choice. I do not want to ever hit you again. You are safe here."

This has no effect on the molly, indeed it isn't even

clear if she has understood Molly. She shrugs, picks up her book, and reads through the noise.

An hour later, the molly is still raging like she's set to pop an artery in her skull, no let-up in sight.

"You are safe. Nobody will hurt you," says Molly. "We can protect you here."

No response.

Molly gets an idea and goes to the kitchen. She makes a sandwich, unimpressive: tomato and cheese. She adds a glass of milk and drops some gin in it.

She brings it back to the room, but the molly is gone.

"Holy fuck!"

Of course she's gone. She must have memories of their mother teaching escape techniques. Molly's knuckles already ache and she doesn't want to have to fight again today.

Fuck. Okay.

"Molina! Ann! She's loose!"

The second thing Molly does is check on Moya. She opens the door to her room and finds Moya on the bed, hooded as usual. The room is dark, also as usual.

"Stay here. The molly is about."

Moya points to a space behind the door and Molly turns.

The girl is unconscious, tied up again, fresh cables.

Molly looks from her to Moya and back again. She yells, "Never mind, girls, false alarm!"

Eleven

Okehampton is so British, it might have been designed by fantasy writers. It has ruins, Okehampton Castle. It has a river that runs through, the Okement, and it was founded by Saxons. Population, five thousand, six thousand, who knows?

Myke emerges from the train station and knows immediately that she shouldn't have left her jeep in Exeter, and that the molly is not in Okehampton. Too few people, too little anonymity.

She knows where this is going. She walks up a crest and looks around. Dartmoor Forest. That's where the duplicate will be. It will have set up camp and be foraging and hunting from there. Lord knows why it killed the man, not that it matters right now.

Big forest, though. Makes sense to go south of the castle, follow the Okement into the forest, which is what the duplicate will do.

First, for completeness, and because she is a professional, Myke will go over the town of Okehampton. She will sit in their pubs, drink their beer, dine, first by herself and then with strangers. She will join in their gossip if she can. She will play the tourist. The town will give up its secrets to her and she will know if the duplicate has been seen there.

A few days later, she will get back on the train to Exeter, pick up her jeep, and drive into the forest. She will find the murder site, take her hiking gear from the back of the jeep, and hunt the clone down.

Satisfied with her plan, she calls Gove. She doesn't know when she'll next be close to a phone booth.

"Do you sleep in the office?" she asks.

"I'm not in the mood, Myke. You will not believe the firestorm of paperwork your little stunt at Colnbrook and Maidenhead has caused. The Woking folks don't seem to mind. I'm not sure why. Where are you?"

"I'll give you a hint. I can see sheep, grass, beautiful rolling hills, and the people are really friendly."

"You're not there to be a tourist."

"That's not entirely true. I have to blend in. This mission does have a covert aspect, right?"

"Just get it over and done with. Oh, and there's been another murder. Two, in fact. Sean and Jane Drake. Married couple. Camping."

"In Dartmoor?"

"Yes. Same modus operandi. They were beaten to death by hand. No sign of the assailant's tracks or spoor."

"Give me a map reference, Gove."

He does.

"Thanks, that's useful."

"Myke, I don't have the juice to keep the locals off the case for much longer."

"You will keep the Keystone Cops off my back, Gove. I don't have time to worry about their feelings."

"If you're fast, I won't have to. I've left a fax for you at the local station. It's on Barton Road. They're expecting you."

"Bye."

"I want daily updates!"

She hangs up. She makes one more phone call, briefer. Then she leaves the phone booth.

Close to the station there's a picturesque little bridge that's right out of a storybook. Myke wouldn't be surprised if trolls lived under it. Thread-like stalactites reach down from it. If signs are to be believed, there's a place she can hire a bicycle.

Twelve

Slightly different tactic this time.

Tamara pores over records of new business registration. The fitness craze of the eighties, since Jane Fonda did her thing, led to the flowering of gyms, first aerobics, then all kinds. The search is enormous, but they can narrow it down to gyms opened or purchased after the last time they saw Molly Southbourne. Those businesses are the only ones worth their attention.

With list in hand, they walk about, watch, wait, interact with the receptionists if need be. Sometimes the owners' photos are in the lobby. Not all the tamaras know what a molly looks like. As a result there are many false alarms. No harm done, they just reset.

One of the tamaras sees someone who might be a molly walk into a gym. She alerts the others, and Tamara, who does know Molly, arrives in her tinted rental and waits. She has another tamara at the back, just in case they've found her.

After waiting three hours, Tamara knows the molly isn't here for a workout. It must be she who owns and runs the place. She sucks on a bottle of orange juice and listens to Teddy Riley. All the tamaras are pretty much New Jack Swing fanatics now.

When the woman emerges Tamara's hair stands on end.

"That's her. That's who we're looking for," says Tamara. She can hear the thud of her heart beating harder. Calm down. Decide what to do with precision, not panic. Funny. She had thought herself over this fear of Molly. Apparently not.

This one has short, punky hair, spiked up with gel, though the rest of her ensemble is relatively tame. Khakis, a plain white T-shirt with no slogan, combat boots. The hair is lighter than Molly's usual jet black. Tamara can't see the eyes from here, but she bets they are blue-gray, darker when angry. And there's the walk. The slight lope that says, I can beat you to death with my pinky; don't fuck with me. Tamara exhales and picks up the radio.

"Everybody back off. We're in a sea of white, can't blend in. Wait till nightfall. Out."

Tamara hunkers down and keeps her eyes on the gym. She sips water and eats cheese and onion crisps. She looks at a map. On the business register, this gym is owned by an Ann Whitlow, no Southbourne in the paperwork. Tamara waits. After opening hours she drives off, parks somewhere she won't draw attention, and returns. The front has a shutter, so Tamara will not be entering that way. There's a diner next door. Security is not nearly as serious as the gym. The buildings aren't terraced, but they are almost in contact. That's the way in. From the back seat she grabs some brown paper bags that make it look like she is either delivering or receiving takeaway. Tamara easily gets into the diner, then up the back stairs onto the roof. The gap is nothing to speak of. She steps from the first floor of one building into the other.

The gym is comprehensive, if nothing else, but it does not interest Tamara that way. She looks through all the mail she can find. She scribbles down addresses. There's a beige computer on the desk, but she is not the tamara with a Computer Appreciation course under her belt.

There are documents for Whitlow, and one of them makes her head explode: Mollyann Whitlow is the full name. Registered disabled.

She senses movement at the window and sees an urban fox out on the street.

She checks her watch.

Time to go.

Thirteen

In the gloom of her room Moya stands in front of her mirror and takes off her hood. She leaves the dark glasses on for now. She picks up the brush and runs it through her hair. It only covers one-third of her scalp on the left side. The rest of her head is smooth with scar tissue. She has no eyebrow on the right side. She brushes her hair lovingly. It is jet black and shines, with full body and a significant bounce when she doesn't tuck it in. She read about brushing a hundred times a night, and she has done that for months now. She applies skin treatment and face cream. She hooks two earrings into the left ear, because she doesn't have a lobe on the right.

She applies lip gloss. She bares her teeth, and they are even, white, perfect.

She takes the glasses off. No normal eyelids on that side.

She applies three kinds of eye drops to her right eye. The lid does not blink, so she needs artificial tears. 0.3% hypromellose. Preservative-free because of how frequently she uses them. She checks for signs of infection.

None. She checks for signs of drying. None.

She replaces the glasses, moisturizes the rest of her skin, sprays perfume.

She tries on a new pair of jeans. She plays music and dances to Bell Biv DeVoe, flinging her head this way and that. She dances every day, and is better than any of her sisters, even Ann. She flops on the bed and listens to *Diary of a Mad Band* on repeat.

Pleasure sinks into her. Life is good.

A screech penetrates her calm briefly, but she knows who it is. The wild molly. Moya rises and pulls her hood over her head, then flits over to have a look.

Ann sits in a rocking chair reading. The molly hisses and strains against her bonds, face red and smeared with food from when they tried to feed her. Bruised where first Molly, then Moya hit her in the noggin.

Moya doesn't feel good about this, although she can't think of any other solution. Captivity isn't cool. All of them have been kept captive at one point or the other. Molly was beaten, then chained down by the original Molly. Molina was held in biological captivity, inside a man who was trying to survive, but didn't. Moya and Ann fought the original Molly as the first act of their lives. Moya has never indicated this to anyone, but it was she who killed the original Molly Southbourne.

She woke, found herself doused with lighter fluid and

petrol—Molly was thorough—in the dark, with several other duplicates. It was a fight from the first. Moya was at the periphery. She saw the original puree the face of one duplicate and make easy work of the others. Working on instinct, Moya grabbed a chair leg—the room was full of broken furniture. The fire had spread, but was still under control. Original Molly was in the process of wrenching Ann's arm in the wrong direction when Moya flew at her with the leg. It was a testament to her skill that Molly turned at the last minute and saw Moya. In that split second she could have countered the descending blow but instead she smiled and closed her eyes. Moya did not hesitate. She beat the monster to death and kept beating her long after her heart must have stopped, and long after she might have reached a safe distance from the fire. By the time Moya realized what was happening her head and body were already burning, and there was no oxygen left. She blacked out and came to in a cage next to Ann, drugged, sluggish, uncomprehending.

Molly saved them, although Moya can't remember the details of that. They slowly detoxed from the drugs Vitali Nikitovich gave them. The first words Ann said to her were "I know you saved my life. I will never forget that."

Moya's sisters all seem to hate the original Molly because of the violence she visited on successive generations of duplicates. Moya figures this is because the object of their hatred is out of reach, already dead. The only reason Moya doesn't share this hate is because she dealt the killing blow. Fuck you, Molly Southbourne. Fuck you and the blood you rode in on.

Moya remembers, and doesn't want to be jailer for anyone.

But the key problem is that this molly should be talking by now. Her memories, Molly's memories, should be coming back to her. It's been a week and nothing has changed. Instinct tells Moya nothing is going to change. This molly will remain feral. The decision ahead of them is whether they keep her against her will or kill her. Letting her go is not an option—she'll just turn around and attack again, trying to get to Molly. Moya cannot be part of any plan that involves killing a molly.

She leaves them alone and zips up her coat. She leaves the house quietly, making sure the door settles into place softly.

It's early evening. She could call a taxi, but she doesn't. She wants to walk. The farther away she is from other people the better. For them. Moya isn't bothered about her scars, but if she can stop people feeling uncomfortable, she will.

She arrives at the Burning Dog pub and scans it from the outside, trying to spot Molina. This is her sister's favorite pub and where she comes to pick up guys and sometimes girls. Moya follows her most times because she might need backup. She doesn't think Molina knows. She's never mentioned it to Moya.

There she is, chatting with a footballer type and drinking a draft of something. From the window Moya can see her altered body language, inviting, seductive. The footballer is responding to it. Which is good. Moya won't have to spend the whole evening skulking. She has been outside for an hour when they move to leave together. Moya sinks into the darkness of the car park. If this is like other times they will leave in the guy's car and Moya will go home. They are kissing now.

Moya is about to leave when she sees . . . a woman.

Someone is following Molina. Not just that, it looks very much like one of the people who guarded Moya and Ann when Vitali held them.

Tamara.

~

The tamara does not directly follow Molina and her footballer. But she does speak into a radio, and a car follows in the same direction as Molina.

Moya isn't sure what to do. She knows she can't let this tamara out of her sight. She knows that Molina might be in trouble. She knows that it might be more useful to find out where the tamaras are based and what their plan is.

Moya follows the tamara, who seems oblivious, a young woman out for a stroll. Moya is extra careful that she is not being flanked or followed by a second tamara that she does not know about. The tamara stops at a shop to buy something. Moya waits. Shops are no good. Cameras. Reflective surfaces. Best to wait.

The tamara comes out with cigarettes, which she lights up as she walks along.

The problem: Moya bears the tamaras a grudge, and right now her feelings are intensely retributive, not strategic. She thinks Molina can take care of herself.

This lone tamara, on the other hand . . .

~

Abandoned building. Many of them in Devon these days. Young people are leaving for places that have jobs. Devon isn't one of them. Tin and copper mining is dead, pottery is no longer a thing, and agriculture remains on precarious grounds.

Moya doesn't tie the tamara down. She tried to run once, and Moya caught her so easily the second time that she seems to have given up.

She knows tamaras carry weapons. She searches for it, finds the handgun, and unloads it, checking the chambered round. She switches the radio off. She frisks the tamara for anything else. Satisfied, Moya writes a message as the tamara babbles about mercy.

When the tamara has calmed down Moya takes off her glasses and pulls down her hood. The tamara cowers and is shaken like most people, and Moya realizes this is not the Prime. The Prime knows about her and Ann.

She hands the written instructions over to shaking hands.

What are you planning to do with my sister?

"Nothing. We're just watching."

Why?

"I don't know."

Moya clenches her fist.

"I don't. Listen, if you are who I think you are, then you know a bit about this. We're not a hive mind. Each person has a duty. Only Tamara knows the whole picture. You can beat on me for as long as you want. It won't get you more information." She spits blood-tinged saliva to her left. It looks like acrylic paint. "I am like you. I won't allow my sisters to come to harm. You'll have to beat me to death, and I'm happy to die for them."

Moya writes, *I'm not going to kill you.*

This is not a lie, but she will use this tamara to send a message, just in case Molina doesn't make it home.

When she's finished, she takes all the identity documents she can find on the tamara and starts home. She does not go in, but waits in the hedges.

A car swings up, a taxi. The door opens and Molina climbs out and pays.

Moya doesn't alert Molina to her presence, but keeps watch on the street, up one way, then the other. Silence. No people, no foxes, no house cats. They didn't follow Molina all the way home.

She waits an hour after she is satisfied, then she goes in.

She takes off her lipstick, changes into sweats, washes her hands, and tapes the cuts. Ann is asleep, and the wild molly is awake, but yawning with heavy eyes.

Moya touches Ann, kisses her forehead, and steers her out.

She sits in the rocking chair and thinks about what to do with the information she has. The molly stares at her.

The night passes.

Fourteen

Sod's Law, it's raining, the annoying kind that starts and stops. When she finishes this assignment, Myke is going on holiday to somewhere warm, where the only umbrellas are the ones on drinks.

She has a thermal dry suit on underneath her other gear, which is a concession to old age. She'll ache in her right sacroiliac joint a week from now, she knows for certain, but for today, she will push herself to find the molly.

The Okement's water level is higher, of course, but nothing that makes Myke think of flooding. She has swum in faster, deeper rivers, but that doesn't mean she shouldn't give it her respect. She keeps it in sight and goes deeper and deeper into Dartmoor. She orients herself with a map reference. The molly won't be on a footpath. Myke isn't moving like a camper or hiker. She is moving between areas that provide cover, like a bush or rock. From there, she stares and listens and stares some more. She slowly surveys her entire visual field, then moves her neck to widen it, until she can say for certain there is nothing suspicious ahead of her. That done, she darts to a new position and repeats. She looks up the trees for a particular kind of spoor. Nothing yet.

She slips and falls. She slides on muddy grass for about half a yard. When she stops, she looks around her and sees why. The area has been denuded. There are flecks of wood on the ground. She picks them up and brings them closer to her eyes—her vision is going too. They are curved, with sharp edges. Shaved off a branch or log. Weapon making. Stakes for camp and for a trap. She looks carefully, but there is nothing else to spot.

She finds the police tracks. They have trampled over everything in their clumsy quest to find the killer by beating the bushes. Idiots. The molly would have heard them coming and hidden, watching them from a distance. They thought they were dealing with some lunatic. Their notes say so. They have no idea.

As she plods on she remembers a film she saw some years back. A space creature hunted US marines in a South American jungle, killed them off one by one. One of them, in frustration, stopped running, dropped all his gear, and decided to face the monster bare chested and with just a hunting knife, mano a mano. At that point Myke checked out of the film. Why do men think this is how fighting is done? Or is it just Hollywood? Never give away your advantage.

She finds something, a depression in the grass. She scrapes away at it and reveals a hastily filled hole. Myke digs in it and encounters fresh shit. Might be other campers, but Myke doubts it. The story of the murder would have spread like a brush fire. The soft-arse campers are all gone. Only the molly and Myke remain.

Myke moves back about a yard, then starts weaving foliage into a covering she brought along, then she sits under it. She can see where the pit was. The molly would be acting like a ranging animal. She'll see this area as where she disposes of her waste. She'll be back to dig another hole. That's what Myke would do if she decided to go feral one day.

Myke waits, with night glasses hanging off her neck.

She is utterly still, even when thunder cracks and lightning flashes. She only moves her eyes, left to right, up and down. Her ears are alert for any sound that is not dripping water. She's hungry and she wants to take a piss and this is the last fucking time she's doing something like this. It's a young person's game. Doesn't matter if you're a yoga master or a Kegel fiend, your bladder isn't the same after fifty.

Jesus, you're soft too.

She spots the molly.

To her left, moving from tree to tree, doubling back on herself, moving in a spiral. Good girl, just not good enough.

Myke raises a tranq gun, slow, *slow*. Not gonna do this hand to hand in the mud with a person in their twenties who is lethal at the best of times. Age may bring wisdom, but it also brings joint wear. Labor-saving devices are essential.

She has the molly in her sights and is about to fire when she hears another sound. Closer. She has enough discipline to remain still and hold her breath. A sudden movement might give her away.

It's another molly, a second one.

What?

This one's moving faster than the first. They're working together. Not a great situation. She may be able to take one out with the tranquilizer, but would she be able to reload before the second was on her? Maybe, but too much uncertainty. Plus, it's wet, slippery. She might not get it done in one. No, change of plans. Besides, if there are two, who's to say there aren't three? Or thirteen? She'll follow at a respectful distance, see where they take her.

The rain stops suddenly, and only the leaves and boughs drip. Both mollies freeze.

Myke's bladder is killing her. The irony is, if she hadn't worn a dry suit, she would have just pissed. They move on. Myke rises, unloads the dart gun, and packs as quickly and silently as she can manage, then goes after the mollies.

~

Full dark. Myke has lost the map reference points. She does not know where she is, but she knows those abominations are ahead of her, the first still using a spiral, the second direct. They aren't hunting; they are traveling somewhere specific.

It's a strange dance. Myke can only move when they move so there's no extraneous noise, and she stops to look when they stop. They all three of them disturb animals, but the scurrying is nonthreatening mammalian survival instinct. They don't seem to be signaling each other, but the second molly clearly takes its lead from the first. Myke tries to look ahead, to find something familiar from her preparation to ground her in place.

The lead molly stops, and the second one catches up. Myke echoes their movements. Now beside each other, the two mollies stare ahead at something, then move as one, disappearing from view.

On cue, the rain starts again.

Myke waits. She checks her compass, waits some more. One of her instructors had been to Vietnam, one of the first batch, and he did three tours. He said the most important part of jungle warfare is waiting. Watching and waiting. That was the key.

Watching and waiting, looking above.

That was from a song, wasn't it? A hymn.

Myke advances carefully. She's looking at the ground with the night vision, trying to anticipate traps, tripwires, anything. She finds the land declines, as if she is going down.

What were they looking at?

She scans and scans, but finds nothing of interest.

They were looking above.

Oh.

She is looking up when the strike hits her. She rolls with it instinctively, going limp, not resisting the force, not feeling the wet forest floor.

Underestimated them. Silly old cow, been out to pasture too long.

She is bleeding, the warmth distinguishing itself from the cold rain.

Well, then. Let's go out in style.

She waits till they are both down from the tree. She has slid three feet from them and is lying on her back, still stunned. At least the blood flows downward from her scalp and not into her eyes.

"Hello, ladies," says Myke. "Love the strategy."

They are silent, not the rage or uncontrolled behavior she had expected.

"Not talking? Oh, well."

She lobs the thermite grenade, which they only see in the last second.

Myke covers her eyes from the flash, and she hears their screams with satisfaction. Intense radiant heat from a fire that lives unbothered by rain. The smell of burning flesh makes Myke's skin crawl. She rises.

One of them is completely destroyed, shriveled carbon lying in a pool of liquefied body fat being the only evidence of her existence. The second appears to have avoided some of it, losing both legs, but still alive and shocked. Myke gently feels her own scalp. It feels tender and boggy. Hematoma. Shit. Still, her dizziness is slight and she seems steady on her feet. She gets the flashlight from her backpack.

She first shines it on the survivor, who is quiet, mostly.

"Look at me," says Myke. "Do you understand words? You should by now. Look at me."

The rain stops.

The molly turns toward her and Myke shines the torch in her own face. "Tell me why you are killing strangers."

The molly squints. "Mother? Ma?"

Myke sees red instantly. She falls to her knees and

starts pummeling the molly. "I . . . am . . . not . . . your . . . mother! I had one daughter, I raised one perfect woman, and her name was Molly Southbourne. You are not my child. You are a nail clipping, you are shed hairs. You . . . are . . . not . . . real!"

When the mist clears the molly is dead, with a bony red pulp where her head used to be. Myke breathes hard and her hands throb with the pain of hitting bone.

"You are not real," she says. "And I am not your mother."

When the rain starts up again, she welcomes it, feels cleansed by it, renewed.

She extracts her shovel and digs a hole. She shoves the remains of the mollies inside. Her boots squelch as she moves around. She drops the backup thermite bomb in the pit and it eats up the last of the duplicates.

If you see yourself, run.

Don't bleed.

Blot, burn, bleach.

Find a hole, find your parents.

The mantra she and Connor taught Molly. The real Molly, her darling daughter.

When the fire burns itself out, she covers the pit with soil and staggers to the river. She has to be careful, she can't afford to fall while she's this groggy from a head injury. Can't fall asleep.

She takes off her clothes, including the dry suit. Naked, she soaks them and scatters powdered bleach over them. She waits till she is satisfied all the blood is dealt with.

Her skin still crawls. She hates when a molly calls her mother.

"Fuck you. Fuck you. You killed Connor. *Fuck you!*"

She screams her incoherent rage into the night, a primal howl she didn't know she had in her.

Fifteen

Ann reads: "*Whitlow. Noun. An abscess or collection of pus in the fingers or toes, close to or associated with the nail bed. See also, whitflaw, which means 'flow.' Middle English. Whit, meaning white, and flaw, which means crack. Also Dutch . . .* do you see what I'm saying, Molly?"

Molly is getting ready for work, trying to decide if she needs an umbrella. "I really don't."

"You named us after a collection of pus," says Ann.

"I named us out of the telephone book, Mollyann."

"But the name means pus in the fingers and toes. Whatever we touch, wherever we go, corruption follows."

"Why are you in my room with a dictionary?"

"Moya has something to say. I'm going to get her to point at words."

"But she can write." Molly stops doing her lashes. "I've seen her write."

"Sure, she can write. In fact, I suspect she can talk. That's not the problem. The problem is not if she can, but if she will."

"Go away, I'm trying to get ready."

"I think what she wants to say is important. You'll want to hear."

"I don't."

"You should. She doesn't do this often."

"Please go away, Ann. Why don't you find Molina for this? It's Saturday. She has no bookkeeping to do on Saturday. The gym, on the other hand, is going to be full. Saturday is Monday to the gym."

"She's sleeping in. She had one of those nights."

"So wake her up afterward."

"Molly—"

"Ann, I love you, but go away."

The TV is on in the lounge, but nobody's watching. Two talking heads, one a Tory MP, the other . . . something not Tory. Apparently the Tory had said something ten years earlier about overpopulation, Malthus, doom and gloom. Now that fertility is all the way down to almost zero per hundred thousand the Not Tory guy is taking Tory MP to task. Ann sweeps past, uncaring, and a flight of stairs takes her to the guest room where Moya waits, hooded like the Grim Reaper.

"Molly has to go to work," says Ann.

Alarmed, Moya shakes her head and rushes past.

The molly on the bed twists and writhes.

"She's wasting her time," says Ann. "I've spent the last century trying to get Molly to come here."

The molly bares her teeth.

"Still not talking, eh? Mind you, Moya isn't the best partner for conversation, if you ask me."

The molly strains to get at Ann.

"You want to fight me? You can't, dude. My kung fu is called the Rotting Hand technique. You want to try?"

The molly squints.

"Never heard of it, have you? It's my own invention. Modified Mantis Style." Ann strikes a pose from the wushu form. The molly isn't impressed.

"I should bring the TV in here. We have videos. Do you like comedies? That's all I watch. I particularly like rewatching *A Fish Called Wanda*. I think good physical comedy like Buster Keaton's oeuvre can be understood universally, don't you? Not a black-and-white gal? Have you seen Jackie Chan's stuff? Ticks the martial arts and comedy boxes at the same time. What's your opinion on Chaplin?"

At least she stops hissing.

"I'll shut up, I promise. But why are you not speaking, sweetie?"

The molly starts her struggle again.

"Right, I'm going to tell you a story about yourself. Well, you're like me, and the story is about me, so it's about you. There was once a girl called Molly who made people when she bled. People like you and me. Those people always tried to kill her, so she killed them, sometimes out of self-defense, sometimes out of necessity, sometimes for sport even. Most of those people were made by accident. I was not. You see, Molly was tired of killing every day of her life, and she wanted to die. It wounded her a little, killed her a little inside. She just wanted the outside to match. She made a whole bunch of us and made us attack her. She was something else, I tell you. Even when she didn't want to live, she was like a whirlwind. I have seen many fighters, but nothing like Molly Southbourne. She tried to wrench my arm off, you know? I passed out from the pain. When I came to, I still had my arm, not this chicken wing, although I had irreparable damage. I was lying there in this burning house, coughing, and these men came creeping around, checking the bodies. They found me and Moya alive, barely. They spoke in Russian to each other, but English to us, which is silly. My mother, Molly's mother, spoke Russian and Ukrainian to us. Anyway, they nursed us to health, then kept us captive. Until our Molly came to liberate us. But we were like you. Can you see where I'm going with this, pumpkin?"

The molly did not.

Ann sits on the bed. "What I'm trying to say is, people like us have a way of becoming disposable. Other people kill us. They kill us because we are many and they are few, and are becoming fewer every day. I don't want you to be killed. I'm going to give you a name. With a name you aren't just that thing in the guest room. My mother called us things. Called us 'it.' Let's see." Ann cocks her head to one side, views the molly from another angle. "Obviously not pretty enough to be an 'Ann.' Heh, geddit? An Ann? No? Tough, tough crowd. How do you like Katharine? Katharine Whitlow. It has a nice ring. Did you know 'Whitlow' means pus in fingers and toes? That's what we're calling ourselves. But Katharine is good. Kathy. I like it. I wish I had a sword. I'd knight you right here. I care not that you are a woman."

Molly bursts in. "We need to wake Molina up."

"Booze night is sacred," says Ann.

Moya floats in and leans against the wall.

"The tamaras are here," says Molly. "That's what Moya was trying to say." She turns to Moya. "And you should totally have told me last night, by the way."

Moya shrugs.

"What do we do?" asks Ann.

"Find them and kill them before they kill us?" asks Molly.

Moya shakes her head.

"No killing," says Ann.

"I warned them. I told them if they came looking for us I would visit vengeance on them."

"Vengeance doesn't always mean killing. Besides, you

know the saying. Seek revenge, dig two graves."

"That's not how it goes."

"You know what I mean."

Katharine rages.

"No progress?"

"She wishes to be known as Katharine from now on. Katharine Pus Flow."

"Shut up about that, Ann, this isn't the time."

"Just saying. What do we do?"

"I'm going to the Burning Dog to ask some questions. Wait here with . . . Katharine?"

"She thinks Kathy's fine."

Molly opens the front door and stops moving. "Somebody wake Molina up."

Ann rushes down and to her side to see what she's looking at.

Oh.

Outside, in the middle of the driveway, hands in the air: Tamara Koleosho.

~

"Do you want some tea?" asks Ann.

"Don't offer her tea. She's come to murder us," says Molina.

"Not murder," says Tamara. "Abduct."

"Fine, abduct. Do you want tea or not?"

"Milk, no sugar."

Molly says nothing, stands at the door, which is still open. Ann knows what she's looking for. The other tamaras. They're out there, without a doubt.

"PG Tips okay?" asks Ann.

"Jesus, Ann," says Molina. "I'll get the tea. She'll drink whatever swill I decide."

Tamara smiles, tight lips. She sits in an armchair, her legs crossed, her bag emptied on the wood panels, her gun in Ann's hand.

"Hi, Molly," says Tamara. "I see you ran with my advice. Good for you."

"Where are they?" asks Molly.

"They're out there," says Tamara. "We're out there. Don't worry about that."

"Why are you here, Tamara?"

"I told you. To kidnap a molly."

"Any molly will do?" says Ann.

Tamara turns to her. "Why? Volunteering?"

"I told you what would happen if you tried this," says Molly.

"And yet here I am," says Tamara. "Stop trying to be threatening, Molly. Sure, you can probably kill me, kill one of us. But I am legion, sister. I always win because I am many. You know this. I know this. Let's get down to discussing why I walked in here. What would you say if I told you Vitali sent me after you?"

"I'd say Vitali is trying to find a way to execute you."

She shakes her head. "Open your mind, Molly."

"Did Vitali pay you to abduct us?" says Ann.

Tamara points to Ann. "Great question. And, yes, he did."

"Why?" asks Ann.

Tamara tells her story.

"I don't get it. Why now?" asks Ann.

"Did you know that Obs-16 has been gutted?" says Tamara. "We've been taking precautions, but they haven't tried to catch or kill us in ages. We are starting to think they're not out there anymore. And if they're not keeping track of . . . us, then maybe Vitali's foreign interests feel emboldened."

Molina brings the tea. Tamara takes a sip and burns her tongue.

"There's sugar in this," says Tamara. Molina gives her the finger without looking in her direction.

"He doesn't want a tamara?" asks Molly.

Tamara puts the tea down. "No. For one thing, that would be too expensive for him. We're in complete harmony. It's difficult to corner and pick off any of us."

"Moya both cornered and picked off one of you," says Molina. "It wasn't hard."

Tamara's face goes hard for a moment. "I got the message she left."

Molina shrugs. "You can come and try your luck when this is all over. Whatever 'this' is."

Ann taps Molina on the shoulder. "Stop." She turns to Tamara. "What is this?"

"This is me saying I will not harm you. This is me saying we are one and the same, and I won't let financial interests come between us."

"What do you want from us?" asks Molly.

"What I've always wanted. Edge. I want your skills to add to our collective knowledge. You started to work with us, but left before we could perfect it. We'd be unstoppable."

"And when you say 'we' this time, that includes us? Because it's hard to keep up," says Ann.

"Yes, this time I'm talking about a partnership of equals."

"What would we do first?" asks Molly.

"We have to neutralize Vitali," says Tamara.

"I thought you weren't killing," says Ann.

"Duplicates. We're not killing duplicates. Humans who endanger us, we kill."

"I'm guessing you have a plan to draw Vitali out?" asks Molina.

"I do. But I need one of you guys."

"Of course you do. How do we know it isn't just a trick to get us to come along quietly? A double bluff," says Molly.

Tamara looks at her wristwatch. "Look outside the window."

"What?" says Ann.

"I'll wait."

Tamaras on the grass, tamaras up the trees, tamaras on the road. At least half armed with pistols.

"I don't bluff," says Tamara. "Single or double or however many multiples you want. I would like us to cooperate and stop the people who want to extinguish us. Are you interested?"

Sixteen

Myke parks the jeep just beside a phone booth that it took hours to find. She made it out of Dartmoor but is so banged up she had to stop at a pharmacy. She built a cairn for the mollies, just in case she has to find them for Gove to verify.

She calls Gove.

"Yes?"

"It's done. There were two of them. You're welcome."

"I don't understand," says Gove.

"I found your errant mollies and I killed them."

A crackle on the line.

"Gove, you don't seem as happy as I would expect."

"Myke, there was another murder today."

"What?"

"I left details at the police station for you. It seems—"

She hangs up and rests her head on the cool alloy of the phone.

How can this be? Why will this strain not just die? When will she be done with this? Has she not paid enough for her sins?

She smashes the phone against the window and keeps whacking it until the receiver comes apart in her hands.

~

She reads the file in the hotel, crammed into the tiny bathtub, washing Dartmoor out of her. The case is certainly suspicious. There is a living witness. The suspected culprit has tangly black hair, pale skin, and wiry muscles.

Killed two people in a boat with her bare hands, not six miles from where Myke is having her bath.

She drops the papers and sinks under the water. This is not ideal. It means she needs to widen her search, and that she doesn't know how many mollies she is dealing with. Neither does Gove, obviously. Completely out of his depth.

Fortunately, Myke has other sources.

She makes a phone call through the switchboard because she just vandalized the booth closest to her.

"Hello?" says the deep voice.

"Hello, Vitali Ignatiy. How are your spleens?"

"Mykhaila Southbourne. It is always a pleasure to hear from you. The spleens have moved on to a happier place. Or so I am told."

"Just like old days."

"Just like old days. What do you need?"

"There are more mollies, Vitali. And I think you know where they are, so don't try to pretend."

"I have always liked your directness, Mykhaila," says Vitali. "You always come to us."

"Just tell me, Vitali. I'm not in the mood, there's a darling."

"You are right, there are more. I am in the process of acquiring them now."

"You only need one, right?"

"I only need one alive," says Vitali. "The situation is dire. There are entire towns with no next generation, where the youngest children are twelve."

"I don't need a pitch. I don't need convincing about your cause, but the idea of those things running around causes an itch in my soul. They killed Connor. They killed Molly."

"Molly killed herself," says Vitali.

"Because of them."

"One might see that as a defect," says Vitali.

"What are you saying?" Myke raises her leg out of the water and studies the moisture wrinkles. She has never known why hands and feet get like that in bathwater.

"There's no point attempting repopulation of a village or town in Karpova or Purnema with a cell line that kills itself, or if the clones have gone Hayflick."

"Hayflick?"

"Hayflick limit. Human cells grown in culture were once thought to be immortal. Leonard Hayflick demonstrated that this was not the case in '61. They divide between forty and sixty times before involuting. After too many generations of duplicates, the products become defective. We called it going Hayflick. You will see mollies that won't remember anything they are taught, mollies that commit murders against random people, mollies that can't be civilized, mollies that rot."

"I'm confused, Vitali. It sounds like you're saying you don't want the mollies."

"I do want them. I do want the one. But I want it as bait."

"Bait for what?"

Vitali laughs. "Have you ever considered the African?"

"Tamara?"

"Yes. We educated her mother, just like we reeducated you, Mykhaila."

The Murders of Mykhaila Southbourne

Somewhere in the USSR, a long time ago . . .

Mykhaila, also known as Michelle White, finishes her psychometric test and puts her HB pencil to the side of the examination sheets. She sits back in her chair and waits.

Vitali comes in with a severe woman in tow. He picks up the pencil and the sheets and hands them to the woman. Then he sits on the edge of her desk.

"Mykhaila. That's your cover name."

"Yes."

"And you say you were sent here by the British government."

"Yes."

"We will check."

"I expect you to."

"How old are you?"

"Eighteen."

Vitali shakes his head.

"Okay, I'm almost seventeen, but I told them I was eighteen."

"I can assure you that they know your true age."

"There's a long history of lying about age to get into armed forces in Britain."

"At wartime."

"I am told this is wartime too."

"What is your mission, little one?"

"Blend in. Become one with the local people. Learn."

"No targets to assassinate or compromise?"

"No such thing."

"Were you trained?"

"I was."

"Weapons?"

"Weapons, communications, munitions, hand-to-hand combat, simple electronics."

"We will test you."

Mykhaila shrugs.

"Why have you surrendered yourself?"

"I spent a week here, with the host family, and I realized something straight away. These people are not my enemy. I don't want to do anything that will harm them."

"So you're defecting."

"No. I want to work for you. I'll submit to a full debrief. Whatever you want me to tell my masters back in Britain I will."

"How do I know this is not just a story you were told to tell us, to get our guard down?"

"Test me. Hypnotize me. Use a lie detector. The works. Do whatever you need to do to get assurance."

Vitali doesn't say anything before he stands up and leaves the room.

~

Someone knocks on Vitali's door.

"Enter."

A uniformed man comes in, but is quiet, his eyes fixed above Vitali's head.

"Well?"

"I think . . . Comrade, you should see this."

"See what?"

"The little English girl, Comrade."

He wants to ask, but instead he rises and follows the recruit to the gymnasium.

Mykhaila is in the boxing ring with two men who are both taller than she. Outside the ring four trainers nurse bruised faces. The two men are closing in on Mykhaila. She doesn't move, although she seems relaxed but alert. They come from both sides, one kicking, one punching. It is unclear what exactly Mykhaila does, but she is swift in a way that makes her movements seem clumsy. The kicking person falls, grabbing his knee, in pain. The puncher falls flat on his face from a trip that Vitali didn't even see. She kicks the back of his head in a playful way, but he was trying to get up, so it's harder than she intended.

"Sorry, sorry! Oops."

She smiles, bright as sunshine.

"Comrade . . ." says the recruit.

"Yes. I know. I expected her to be soft too."

The next two trainers go in the ring, but everybody knows they have nothing to teach this woman. Girl. Maybe they have to learn from her.

"Where did you say you trained?" asks Vitali.

"Scotland. From commandoes. Then some visiting CIA folk," says Mykhaila.

"You have mastered this," says Vitali. "Being here is a waste of your time."

"Not really. I needed a workout."

"Don't show off."

~

The shooting and comms testing goes the same way. Mykhaila breezes through the lie detector with no signs of distress. If she's lying she deserves an Academy Award.

"Why are you so cheerful?" asks Vitali. "Your world has been upended."

"I was serious before," she says. "Super-serious operative, took my studies and my training serious, didn't have fun. The CIA guy told me something. He said I may slip in and find the KGB waiting for me in East Germany. He said you all would torture me, take me behind the building, and execute me. He said to take on this assignment I would need to assume I was already dead."

Vitali nods. "Wise advice."

"He also said you guys have the best vodka, and that Russians can drink. I've yet to see proof of that."

"Everything in its time. And you are underage."

"Shoot me now, please."

"You can have kvass. Good for you. Russian folk drink for all ages."

~

Mykhaila struggles to stay awake as the professor drones on.

"The spleen, like other organs, has stroma and parenchyma. The stroma is the reticular connective tissue that forms a matrix for the parenchyma. There are trapped blood cells and immune cells. Now, the splenic sinusoids are really exciting . . ."

Later, when Vitali reviews her notes after she has gone, Mykhaila has drawn the professor with a gigantic erection tenting his trousers and written: *WHY DO I NEED TO KNOW THIS????*

He smiles.

~

Vitali speaks to his supervisors.

"She's healthy. She's motivated. She has physical skill that I have never seen before, a natural aptitude joined with superb training. Watching her fight is like listening to Stravinsky. Imagine if we had an entire army of her."

"And you think this process can succeed in doing that?"

"We can try."

~

Mykhaila lies on a surgical bed along with sixteen other girls. They look at each other nervously. There's a Persian girl and an African, but the rest seem to be white Russian.

The needle is gigantic and it's going through the skin of the belly directly into the spleen, which, because of the lectures, Mykhaila knows how to locate.

One of the girls says, "For Mother Russia," and all the others laugh at her.

It hurts, but Mykhaila keeps her pain inside, hidden.

~

She has a fever and vomiting for five days. Aside from the

nurses, only Vitali comes to see her. They all wear protective masks, which she later finds out is for her protection because she is vulnerable to infections. Gone are those immune cells that mature in the spleen.

"Malenkaya angliiskaya devochka," he says. "Do not die. We have many important things to do together."

"Vodka. I want to taste some before I die, Comrade Vitali."

"A drop of vodka will kill you right now. Rest."

The nurses take a blood sample and give it to him.

~

She wakes up healthy one day, her recovery sudden and complete. She feels rested, hungry, and dry. No sweat anywhere. She is wearing a shapeless hospital gown and lying in the dark.

She presses the button to summon the nurse.

Standing at the foot of the room is a girl that looks exactly like her. The girl has a fixed stare and breathes in and out like ... a toad? It looks grotesque, but Mykhaila cannot say on what level. She is like a twin, after all.

Mykhaila leaps out of the bed and attacks the girl, efficiently, coldly.

By the time the nurses rush in, the duplicate is lying

with her neck at a lethal angle, chest unmoving.

They admonish Mykhaila and inject her with something that puts her out like a light.

~

When she wakes, there is no duplicate. A surgeon checks her belly and nods.

"I will need to take some blood," she says.

"Of course," says Mykhaila.

"Why did you kill?"

"I thought it was a dream," says Mykhaila. "I was confused. You should have warned me."

~

It's worse the next time. This meeting is set up formally, with bodyguards in the hospital day room.

The clone is docile until she sees Mykhaila, and then she goes berserk. She kills both guards, takes their truncheons, and comes for Mykhaila like she can remember the last murder. She doesn't quite have the skills and Mykhaila is able to disarm, disable, and kill her.

Vitali rubs his temples.

~

Every single duplicate tries to kill Mykhaila.

They try everything: soothing music, meditation, various dietary contrivances, tranquilizers. Mykhaila and her clones will not play together.

Three girls survived, apart from Mykhaila. The others died in the days after injection.

"I have some rules for you, Little English Girl. First, try not to bleed. Second, if you do bleed, soak it up and douse it in bleach, or burn it. Third, if you ever see someone like you coming, run away. We don't think it's a good idea for you to keep killing someone that looks like you."

"I don't have a problem with it."

"You say that now. But our psychiatrist thinks over time it will be a problem."

"You sound disappointed, Vitali."

"This is not what I had hoped for, but it's not your fault. There is some kind of generational memory that we had not anticipated. We're lucky that a space flight accident is drawing attention from this project."

"What's next?"

"Do you play chess?"

"... Should I?"

"Yes, you should. I will teach you. But here's what I know. We cannot solve this problem ourselves. Maybe there's a way of using East and West brainpower in parallel. I want you to contact your handler and tell him everything we did here, except say it was against your will."

"*What?*"

"Think, Mykhaila. If the British have your cells, they'll give them to the Americans. Between the two of them and Canada, they'll reverse engineer the problem to death, work out the bugs, and perfect it. Then we steal the process back, improved, and take the credit."

Mykhaila protests, but the contact is made and she is extracted posthaste.

~

Back in the UK they take Mykhaila's spleen out, then they send her to the South Midlands to recuperate and rejoin society as Michelle White. She compromises and calls herself Mykhaila White. She lives a shell-shocked life, unsure of what she has achieved, still relatively young and with no family to speak of.

The government pays her, and keeps an eye on her. After the splenectomy, she expects her blood to be normal, so she is surprised when she finds a hole in her flooring one morning, and a duplicate smashing her head against the bedpost.

Each copy of her is more difficult to beat than the last. They are learning skills, gaining memories.

The first time, she calls her handlers and they come

and take the body away.

The next time they give her a new number to call.

~

She learns bookkeeping and gets a job at a local newspaper. She is anonymous. She has done nothing of significance but spread violence. Her Russian contacts keep out of sight, but she knows they are there, and even imagines she spots them sometimes.

For three or four years, she never has to call the number, then one afternoon, she's picking up her milk and a duplicate pounces on her. She has to stab it in the neck with a broken milk bottle. They clean it up quietly, efficiently. They take the body away.

They don't explain how she made a duplicate without a spleen, which she's kind of angry about because they told her she wouldn't miss it at first. "The spleen isn't *for* anything." Excuse me, what about all those immune cells?

Turns out not having a spleen makes her vulnerable to infections by encapsulated organisms. Delicious. She has to take regular penicillin injections like a syphilitic sailor. Much later there'll be Pneumovax, but for now, penicillin V.

Once they've gone she realizes she has no milk. She knows it comes from Southbourne Farm, which is just outside town. She needs to stretch her legs and get out of the house since the attack. She drives up to the farm. There, she meets Connor Southbourne.

Lanky, exceedingly calm, forehead like a cliff, hooded eyes, and a soft brogue that Mykhaila didn't know she wanted until she met it.

"You can get milk in the shops, you know," says Connor. "I know there are shortages where you come from."

"I'm British. I've been away."

"Well, prove it. Come in and have a cuppa."

She does. And never leaves.

They talk, and she falls into his eyes, and he hers. It's a farm, so he soon has to leave her and do farming shit, feeding animals, taking away droppings and whatnot. Getting milk right from the udders. Mykhaila waits. She drinks a lot of tea and reads a lot of tractor magazines. Who knew such a thing existed? When he returns they talk about his plays, about living in Dublin briefly, about his mother.

Over lunch, she tells him her mother abandoned her and she was moved from orphanage to orphanage. She doesn't like to remember it. She tracked her mother down when she was fifteen, saw her, but didn't talk to her.

She reads his plays while he goes back to farming. They are dreadful. She does not plan to tell him, but he knows. "They're really bad. I'll never get anything staged, but I enjoyed writing them. And it's not this longing in my heart that I have some unrealized talent. My talent was fully realized."

And bed.

And they are married.

And goes well until she gets pregnant.

She has nine months to tell him about the USSR mission and what she has done. She doesn't. She nests. She does those things you do when you're bringing new life in, and if she's ashamed of being a double agent, she doesn't show it.

The birth itself isn't too difficult. Twelve-hour labor, a private midwife on the farm. Molly comes to the world with a brief squall, then nurses minutes later.

That night, they both hear crying that's not coming from Molly. Outside, where the afterbirth was disposed of, there are two babies, identical to Molly, with no belly buttons.

"Who are they? Mykhaila, what is this?"

"Go back inside," she says. "I'll explain everything. But first I want you to know that whatever I do tonight, and from this day forth, it's to protect our daughter. Say you'll understand."

Connor nods, lingers a second or two, then goes inside.

She thinks about it first. She could just bring them up alongside her daughter. Nobody would know and maybe they won't try to kill Molly. But she wouldn't know for sure and . . . there's no way to chance that. There's no option. It would always be a possibility that they could turn one day and since Mykhaila would never know, she would never rest. She would always wonder, live her whole life on alert. No. This ends now.

"I'm sorry," she says to the uncomprehending clones. "I'm so sorry."

She remembers the rules Vitali gave her and implements them.

She spends all night talking to Connor.

He has questions, she answers them. He doesn't comment on her actions. He asks how this will work going forward.

Subsequent . . . neutralizations are easier than the first one. They hurt a little less each time, and the clones are always a little older, which makes it more bearable than when they were squalling cherubs.

She has to teach Molly how to defend herself. She'll have no proper childhood, just combat. She must make her stronger. I'm sorry.

When the clones start coming for Molly, when she starts walking, Mykhaila protects her child effectively. By this time any remorse is long dead. Molly's blood produces clones at an exponential rate, much more than Mykhaila's occasional affair. Mykhaila makes one a year, at most. She never discusses it with Connor; besides, their lives are consumed with Molly and the farm.

She watches the child grow. When she says she wants to go to university Mykhaila is apprehensive, but knows it is inevitable. She has done her best to bring the girl up. Her daughter will have to sink or swim. She has the tools to survive.

At first she does nothing, but the suspense grows unbearable. After a month, Mykhaila goes to the university to trail her own daughter. She checks out all Molly's associates and follows them, goes into their residences, drinks their milk. She finds nothing to concern herself over.

She returns to Southbourne. There is no point monitoring everything.

She writes journal entries, and fake letters to Molly explaining her condition. Not truly fake, just full of falsehoods that hold a symbolic truth. In her journals, she writes the truth. The factual truth.

My name is Mykhaila Southbourne, and I have the honor to know that when I die, it will be at the hand of my daughter, Molly.

This would not be a bad death, and I am not upset. I have faced death before, and perhaps the reason I have never fallen is I haven't seen a worthy cause of a good death. I simply refuse to succumb to mediocre fatality.

To die, to be killed by Molly, a weapon I perfected, this would be a good death.

It's not like she hasn't tried to murder me before.

~

Southbourne Farm, at night, asleep beside my lover and husband, Connor Southbourne. I am lost in the depths of sleep, dreaming of axes and the chopping of wood, lulled by Connor's breathing no doubt.

Something changes in the room and my eyes open. I roll off the bed to the carpet just as I hear the whuft of impact, a solid object landing where my head was.

There are three of us in the room now. A part of me notices that I can't hear Connor breathing, but I shove that out of my mind. I bottom-shuffle toward the wall until my back meets resistance. Once I get my bearings I push myself up till I'm standing. A shadow in the dimness, coming toward me, weapon in hand.

I am nowhere near a light, but I don't need it. I have fought people blindfolded in my time and I know my way around this room.

The shadow raises the weapon. It has gawky, ungainly movements, though silent. It's a molly, of course. Still, it seems I have hours before it brings its arm down in a strike. I hit its weapon arm at the elbow and shoulder, and the plank clatters to the ground. I punch it in the center of the chest and bring my knee up to the pit of its belly. The forced exhalation is fetid. Everything about this molly smells disgusting and I almost don't want to touch it to end its life. Almost.

I kick it, intending to sweep it to the ground, but its leg breaks and it screams. Second try, it's on the ground, right leg at an abnormal angle. My knee in its back, I pull on its head and snap the neck.

Must be malnourished for the bones to break so easily.

It twitches for a longer time than I would have thought, but it's been a long time since I killed someone, maybe a year or even two.

It is still.

I check its weapon. Nails in the wood. I touch them, and there is wetness on the iron. Oh, shit.

On the bed I find what I suspect. It's Connor's blood.

And Connor is dead.

~

Most people, on discovering their spouse murdered in the night, would probably break down and cry for a time, then call the police or someone they trust. I am not most people, I don't cry, and I am the one that I trust. Fuck the police.

I head to the basement, to a part of the house nobody goes to. I have to move bric-a-brac, but I finally find it: a deep freezer. I was last here seven years ago; Molly was still home, but even she doesn't know about it, which is saying something because that girl got everywhere. I'm glad she's off to university because this would be twice as hard if I had her underfoot.

I unlock the padlock and open the lid.

Inside, curled up, naked and peaceful, not a mark on her, is a duplicate of me.

~

Naively, I think this is the last trauma I will inflict on Molly.

I leave Connor where he died, though I stare a long time. I will need to remember the image later when I have the luxury to mourn. So long, my love, you did not deserve this or any of the carnage I brought on your head. Beside him, in my bedclothes, I place my dead duplicate. I've cut her hair to match mine, dressed her in my clothes. It doesn't matter that she is stiff from the freezer, by the time she is discovered it won't matter.

Nothing matters.

I pack a bag. All of Mykhaila Southbourne's identification documents are still here, passport, driver's license, tax returns. I have others, which means I can shed Mykhaila like a snake does its skin.

I don't call the number that is rapid-cycling in my brain. This is the very situation it exists for, but that's for them, not me. They will come eventually, and they'll think the molly killed us both, Connor, with ease in his sleep, me, with great difficulty. They'll think I succumbed to injuries after killing the assailant. It'll break Molly's heart, but she'll get over it. Maybe this is best.

I walk out of the door, but I hear a groan.

That manky molly is still alive. She can't survive long, though. She was already skinny and starved.

I hesitate for a few seconds, but the moment passes and I continue on, into the sunrise.

~

That was the last murder of a duplicate Mykhaila remembers. She remembers burning the journals and changing towns. Shortening her name to Myke, which is disorienting to people, but not too much. It is apparently a modern thing to adopt variant spellings of traditional names.

Gove helps her relocate, and she has been fine since then. Until now.

The water is cold. Myke pulls the plug and steps out.

She is unsatisfied with the bath, but that's because of Vitali's news.

At least now she has a plan. And after this, her hatred of all mollies sated, she will disappear. She has no further interest in becoming anything or achieving anything other than vengeance for Connor.

And this is how it will go: all mollies will die.

Tamara is the future.

Makes sense.

Seventeen

Tamara is interrupted by her radio. "Excuse me," she says, and moves to a corner.

Molina and Ann look to Molly. "I'll go," says Molly. "It can't be you, Ann, and I don't even know if Vitali knows about you, Molina."

"I don't think that's a good idea," says Molina. She raises her hands in a peace gesture. "Not just because I like to disagree with you, honest. Look at the wild molly."

"Kathy," says Ann.

"Kathy. She won't be the only one out there. There's a remnant and they're looking for you as their Prime. If you're not here, if you die, what happens to them?"

"I . . . What are you saying here?" asks Molly.

"We have to find and protect our sisters who are still out there, give them sanctuary."

"Even if they're going to slit our throats first chance they get?" asks Molly.

"I was going to slit your throat the first chance I got. Look at where we are now," says Molina.

"This remnant you speak of is theoretical. Kathy might

be the only one left," says Molly.

"I don't think that's a logical or safe position to take," says Ann.

"I agree," says Tamara. "Guess what? You have incoming mollies."

~

From the roof you can see the rolling hills and undulations of Devon for miles around the house. It's isolated, which is one of the reasons the house was cheaper and the main reason Molly bought it. Molly and Tamara sit side by side, careful not to slide off.

It's not too windy and the sky is clear.

"Perfect day for a massacre," says Molly. "Perfect day to die."

"Are you married to this no killing idea?" asks Tamara. "We have guns. It might even the odds."

Molly turns to her. "Then you can leave. Nobody kills them. You kill a molly, you have to answer to me, Tamara."

"You may not remember that we have died to keep you alive."

"I do remember and I'm grateful, but you heard my sisters. They feel quite strongly about it, and I have to respect that."

"We're not leaving."

Molly looks at the trees and the rustling of grass and the shaking of the bushes. She can't see any mollies advancing.

"Can't we just kill them a little bit?" says Tamara.

"Tell me where they are."

"They're still too far out, but they are definitely coming here."

"How many?"

"Seventeen so far."

"How fit are you?"

"I just finished the Hundred-Man Kumite, by which I mean I didn't finish."

"Oh, you went back to karate."

"Yeah. I'll finish it one day."

"If you can finish the kumite, then surely you can knock out seventeen mollies."

"Can I shoot them in the leg?"

They hear the doorbell. Both scramble back in through the dormer window that led them up in the first place.

Dr. Ling is at the door.

"Hello," she says.

"Dr. Ling, it's Saturday. You can't be here. Did we have an appointment?" asks Molly.

"I was in the neighborhood and decided—"

"This isn't on the way to anywhere, Doc. You couldn't have been in the neighborhood."

She looks uncomfortable and fidgets with her glasses.

Tamara draws a gun. "Can I at least kill her? She's shady."

"She said she'd kill my children," Dr. Ling blurts.

"Who?"

An explosion flings them all to the ground and breaks the front windows. The shock wave blows the door right off the hinges and hits Ling in the back. Molly and Tamara are already flat.

Molly peeps through the doorway. The doctor's Fiat is on its side in flames. No bad guys in sight.

Tamara's radio squawks. She talks into it in short bursts. "The doctor came alone, but they suspect an accomplice. The two tamaras sent to find out haven't returned, or checked in."

"Mollies?"

Tamara shakes her head. "This isn't the mollies' style. They don't even use guns."

"Just what we need," says Molly. "Help me get the door off Ling."

Molina comes down the stairs with a gym bag. Between the three of them they get the doctor to the sofa.

"We should put her in with Kathy, then secure the room," says Molina.

"There's a Kathy? Who's Kathy?" asks Tamara.

"Not now."

From the bag Molina selects and tosses knuckle wrapping, which Molly snatches out of the air and puts on. Molina straps on shin guards and offers them to Tamara, who shakes her head. Mouth guards, Molly slips in her pocket. Moya comes downstairs hooded and starts to gear up from the bag.

"I've put in all the plastic ties I can find," says Molina. "Subdue and restrain."

"Subdue and restrain," says Tamara into the radio. "No guns. But defend yourselves. We're not here to die for the mollies." She looks into Molly's eyes when she says this.

"Guys," says Ann from the landing. "Come check Kathy out."

~

Kathy opens and closes her mouth soundlessly, slowly. Her eyes have gone filmy and do not appear to focus. Her movements are sluggish, and she writhes as if in pain. There are black blotches on her skin.

On the other side of the room, Dr. Ling is awake, but seems confused. A line of blood tracks down from her right ear. "What's going on here?"

"Doctor, we may have left a few things out of our family history," says Molina. "Sorry."

"Never mind her, what's with the molly?" asks Tamara.

"Kathy."

"Right. What's wrong with her?"

"Is she . . . dying?" asks Molly.

"She's definitely sick," says Ann. "But that's not the pressing problem, I think. Look."

There are mollies on the lawn. Four of them, heading for the house with ratty hair and evil intent.

"I'm going out there," says Molly. "Barricade the house."

"Why would you go out?" asks Molina.

"I'm the one they want. Maybe I can lead them away from you lot," says Molly. She tries to leave, but Molina grabs her arm.

"Don't die," she says. She kisses Molly on the lips.

~

The back door slams behind Molly and Tamara. The mollies aim for them.

"Hundred-Man, eh," says Molly.

"Yep," says Tamara.

"If you survive this it'll be a cakewalk." Molly puts her mouth guard in.

"See you on the other side," says Tamara.

At first it seems like she will collide with the first

molly, but Molly avoids her at the last minute, coils herself around the duplicate, and gets on her back. She kicks her knees and takes her down to the grass, tying her up before the next one can close. She rolls, knowing they'll almost be on her. She comes out with an uppercut that lands squarely on a jaw, and the molly's eyes roll up. She drops. Molly spins and her hook kick hits the molly on the temple. The head wrenches around so loosely that Molly fears she has killed the duplicate. She ties them both up, looks to Tamara, who has finished with her first opponent and is ready to advance.

"Do you notice anything about these mollies?" asks Tamara.

"They stink?"

"Yeah, but they have blotches like Kathy did."

It's true. "Are they all dying?"

Eighteen

The Africans are harder to kill.

Myke is surprised at how well they work together. They almost read each other's minds. But a stun gun is a stun gun. She doesn't want to kill them, she has no quarrel with Tamara Koleosho. As long as they don't get in the way of her eradicating the molly duplicates, Vitali can have one of them for all she cares.

She can see the smoke of the bombed car, and weaves through forest to get there. The front door is off, and all the windows of the façade are gone. She can hear sounds of conflict from the other side, behind the house.

What else have you kept from me, Vitali?

Hands grab at her from behind. She turns to meet them. Tamaras. They have clubs and bare hands, three of them. Tamaras. All right. Myke crouches in a boxer's stance, and takes a club hit on the arm to close the distance and snatch the weapon. She cracks a knee, spins, and crashes down on one's head. Limp. Myke takes a punch to the jaw, rolls with it, receives kicks to her midsection, then a club to her temple.

Two come from both sides at the same time. Myke hasn't done this in a long while, but it's muscle memory. At first she makes the mistake of fighting on their terms, hitting both alternately. But this is a rookie mistake. You fight one, you keep the other at a distance with feints. She hits back harder than she intended because she is angry with herself and knocks one of them out with a single kick to the angle of the jaw.

"Back up, back up!" says the second.

"No," says Myke. She unleashes a flurry of blows, punishing her, and brings down the club again and again.

It occurs to her that the tamara might have been calling for backup. Oh, well. It didn't come.

~

She steps in the house, but finds the antechamber barricaded. Do they know she's coming? No, they know *someone's* coming.

You and your daughter left a number of those things on the English countryside. They're defective but they're still looking for your daughter to kill her. They'll find the next best thing. That's where Tamara is, and that's where they all will be.

She hates going into houses she doesn't know. She unslings her bag and drops it at the entrance. She slips weapons into her waistband.

She searches, nobody on the ground floor. She can see trussed mollies on the lawn outside. Noises coming from further out. She'll get to those later.

She climbs the stairs.

She hears groaning and follows the sound. It's from a closed room. When she opens the door, she knows it's a mistake. She takes in a molly tied up, the doctor cowering, and the attack comes from behind her like she figures. She is already dropping, so it's only a glancing blow. She unsheathes her hunting knife just as the hooded person drops on her. The gut wound is almost an accident. Almost. The first three stabs were definitely accidents.

She pulls off the hood. It's a molly, still alive, but hideously scarred. Blood coming out of it in gouts.

Don't bleed.

Blood lands on her. She just has to hope these creatures don't make duplicates, otherwise this job will take months.

"Mother?"

Myke turns and fires her gun in one smooth motion, lighting up the corridor with each shot. The molly goes down, dropping a bowler hat of all things.

"I am not your mother, you walking crime against humanity," says Myke as she shoots it again. "I am the opposite of a mother to you. I never brought you life. I am the anti-mother, the one who gives you death."

A scream, another molly. Her gun jams, her knife is inside the grotesque. She goes on the offensive, but this one, who has only one good arm, swings Myke around in a smooth motion and throws her down the stairs.

Fuck.

Myke has to admire the technique even as she cracks ribs and strains her neck on the way down. She stops at the landing. Everything hurts. Tries to stand, succeeds, but can't inhale all the way.

There's more stuff in her bag. She moves toward it, but hears a shot and is spun round by an impact. She falls supine and sees the doctor at the landing with Myke's own gun.

Fuck you, I should have killed your children.

Myke needs to retreat. Losing blood now.

A shadow falls over her, and a second.

She looks up.

Two women.

"A molly and a tamara," says Myke.

"You mean *the* tamara," says Tamara.

"And *the* molly." The duplicate points a gun. "Good-bye, Ma."

The sight of a muzzle, that dark hole, the gun sight, shaking.

"My Molly would never shake like that, you shit.

Svolach, you are a pale copy. Kill me already, suka," says Myke.

The molly steps closer. "You made your Molly into a psychopathic killer, and she died because she had some humanity left in her. Which is amazing because you had none to give. Die."

Myke knows nothing after the flash.

Nineteen

It's sunny, so bright the eyes hurt even with sunglasses. No breeze.

Ann says words that Molly can't bring herself to utter. Moya, with a burst of shiny hair and wearing a half mask that she crafted herself. No more hoods. She has Molina's *Golconda* bowler hat clutched in front of her.

On the gravestone: WE ARE NOT IDENTICAL.

"I miss you," Moya whispers.

These are the first words anyone has heard her say and they all crowd around her and hug.

Nobody disagrees with me anymore, thinks Molly.

Twenty-six tamaras shuffle about, not knowing whether they should join the hug. Some of them hold hands.

Molly touches the gravestone, leaves her flowers, allows herself to cry.

Ann reads a narrative poem-essay by Claudia Rankine, something she says was Molina's favorite, but Ann is unreliable with this kind of thing. More likely it's something she likes right now and wants to read.

Molly turns to the stone in the plot next to Molina's. It says:

WE ARE MOLLY SOUTHBOURNE.

REMEMBER US.

~

Molly's phone rings and it's Tamara calling from Lagos.

"Am I too late?" she asks.

"No, there are many of you here," says Molly. "I'm touched, considering you never knew her."

"I want you to meet someone," says Tamara and hands the phone to someone.

"Hello?" Thick accent. "My name is Keji Koleosho. I'm Tamara's mother."

"Good afternoon," says Molly.

"I know this is awkward, but my daughter told me about the horrors you experienced, last year, and all your life. I knew your mother from St. Petersburg a long time ago."

Molly's mouth is dry.

"If you ever want to know about her, I'll be glad to share. You don't have to, because of painful memories, but it's family history. You may have to pass it on one day."

"Thank you for your kind offer. I can't—"

"Of course not. But I'm here if you need me. I'll give the phone back to Tamara."

"Wait. I . . . Did you make duplicates?"

"My duplicates lived for about an hour, then they died."

Tamara comes back on. "Sorry."

"It's all right. I might want to talk to her again."

"Any time."

"Still building a town?"

"Helping. I have the workforce."

"How many tamaras?"

"A hundred and counting."

"Hundred-Woman Kumite. You are amazing women," says Molly. "I have to go."

Gove is standing by the car.

"What do you want?" asks Molly.

"This is . . . odd. I wanted to reassure you that all the molly genetic material has been destroyed. Vitali and parts of his circle have been taken in, but I'll be honest, it is likely they'll be used as bargaining chips for prisoner swaps. It's not justice."

"I'm reassured. Bye-bye."

"One other thing, Molly. I have been asked to offer you a job."

"I own a business. I don't need a job."

"Hear me out. Would you like to teach our agents? It would be part-time and you could formulate your own timetable."

"I don't know what Dr. Ling would say, but, and I'm just guessing here, I think she'd say I need to close that chapter of my life. So, no."

"Sessions going well, I take it?"

"Now that she knows the truth, has lived that truth, we're on a better footing. And it helps."

Gove nods. "All right. If you change your mind."

"I won't."

~

Molly opens her journal and writes.

The house is back to normal, although, what is normal without Molina? The scientists have figured it out. How to induce limited duplication in subjects. It's been done in controlled conditions to a limit of four duplicates. They want to roll out full human testing. They wanted to call it the Southbourne Effect, but I asked them to honor the scientists instead. Or Tamara. When I think about it, she is the full and perfect manifestation of the process.

I have enough journal entries for a book now. I don't

know what it means or if anyone would read it for any reason other than puerile voyeurism.

Maybe it needs to exist as a book, maybe not, time will tell.

All I know is now . . . now, I can bleed.

Afterward/Afterword . . .

In 2004, on the fourth of July, Naomi Ali became the first woman to complete the Hundred-Man Kumite, in Sydney, Australia. She was one of the inspirations for the Molly Southbourne character.

About the Author

Carla Roadnight

TADE THOMPSON is the author of the Molly Southbourne trilogy, the Rosewater novels, *Making Wolf,* and *Far from the Light of Heaven.* He has won the Arthur C. Clarke Award, the Nommo Award, and the Prix Julia Verlanger, and been a finalist for the John W. Campbell Award, the Locus Award, the Shirley Jackson Award, and the Hugo Award, among others. He was born in south London but considers himself a citizen of the world. He lives and works on the south coast of England.

TOR·COM

Science fiction. Fantasy. The universe. And related subjects.

*

More than just a publisher's website, *Tor.com* is a venue for **original fiction, comics,** and **discussion** of the entire field of SF and fantasy, in all media and from all sources. Visit our site today—and join the conversation yourself.